The Mothers
OF COUNTRY DAY

ARLENE MATTHEWS

ISBN: 1467909076
ISBN-13: 9781467909075
LCCN: 2011960513
CreateSpace, North Charleston, SC

For Adelaide Moskowitz,
my fourth grade teacher,
wherever she is...

CHAPTER 1:

Back to School

Let's face it: a lot of days that start out badly just keep getting worse. Maybe it's fate, or an unhappy coincidence. Or maybe it's your attitude, wearing your mind down into a negative groove that attracts troubles the way a freshly washed windshield attracts bird droppings. But not all bad days go downhill. Once in a while you wake up overdrawn at the bank to find a check in the mail, or you wake up alone and end up in the arms of a devoted new lover. And once in a while, though the odds are surely against it, you start off your day a social outcast and end up smack on top of the "A" list.

• • •

In the parking lot of Little Fawn Country Day School, you can't swing a cat without hitting a BMW convertible. Most of the Beamers are parked slightly askew by newly anointed seventeen-year-old drivers with better things to do than worry about staying in the white lines. In the midst of this vehicular jigsaw puzzle, Josie Messina gingerly opened the door of her Cooler at the Shore catering delivery van, keeping one eye on the shiny Z4 Roadster that flanked her left side and the other eye on her apparently frozen twelve-year-old son in the passenger seat.

"Torre," she said in as gentle a tone as she could manage, "scoot on out. Come on, but do it slowly. Watch your door, okay, Shortcake?"

"Mom, don't you know a sign from the universe when you get one?" asked the boy, rolling his bespectacled eyes skyward.

Josie sighed and slumped. Leaving her door ajar, she let her head flop against the headrest. The truth was she'd been thinking the very same thing.

According to the form sent by the school's transportation concierge, the Little Fawn school bus was supposed to pick Torre up at 6:55 a.m. for his first day of seventh grade. Josie had set her alarm for 5:45, allowing enough time to make his favorite breakfast of blueberry pancakes and bacon and to make sure he met the school's dress code—khaki slacks, Oxford shirt, tie, and blue blazer—to the letter. She'd haunted Kohl's all summer, pouncing on those special sales previews they offered their charge card customers until she'd assembled the perfect wardrobe. Now the trick was to pay off her charge card before interest started accruing. That was the thing about department store charge cards, Josie knew: they lured you in with deep discounts, but you could probably get a better interest rate from the Mafia.

Josie had awakened Torre more than an hour before his scheduled pick-up because she knew it would take him time to tie his tie—an art he had recently learned from a YouTube video, a convenient paternal surrogate for fatherless boys everywhere. To make sure her son looked as presentable as possible, she'd lured Newton, their perennially shedding dog, into her bedroom with a biscuit and shut him in despite his outraged whimpers at being so shamelessly duped. They had rescued Newton from the local animal shelter three years ago, and though they never knew exactly what breeds colluded in his mixed blood, telltale blond fluff balls that clung relentlessly to their every item of clothing attested to a mix that seemed part golden retriever, part sheepdog, and part Velcro. But today, Josie resolved, there'd be nothing to mar her son's appearance. She'd even managed to prevent Torre from getting blueberry stains on his crisp white shirt by insisting on draping a dishtowel over him while he ate.

Watching him at the kitchen table wearing the makeshift bib, she had just about burst into tears. Part of her was overwhelmed with pride that her amazing math wizard of a child was actually going to be attending Little Fawn Country Day School on a full tuition scholarship, and part of her was panic-stricken about how fast their time together was going by. It seemed like mere days ago that her double-dimpled toddler had sat at that same table in a high chair, clutching a wooden Thomas the Tank Engine train in his right hand and aiming spoonfuls of banana-flavored oatmeal in the general direction of his mouth with his left hand. Now and again he'd miss the mark and wind up with a gooey glob of cereal in his wild, curly hair. His hair had grown from three separate crowns on his scalp, and that gave him the appearance of being something of a mad scientist in the making.

At age twelve, Torre's light brown locks were still so unruly that Josie had surreptitiously placed some of her styling mousse in the palm of her hand this morning and given him a seemingly benign pat on the head for encouragement. She'd hoped for the best as he stood at the front door waiting for the yellow bus that would transport him into a new and different world—at least for seven and a half hours a day.

But the bus never came.

By 7:05, Josie was nervous. By 7:15, she was near frantic. Was there some mistake? It had been six months since Dr. Preston Nobler, the headmaster of Little Fawn Country Day, had contacted her. He'd been at an awards ceremony where Torre had received recognition for earning the highest standardized test math score in the county. Dr. Nobler had told her, off the record, that he'd heard it was in fact the highest score in the entire state of New Jersey. He'd wanted to get to know Torre, he'd said—such an outstanding young man. Then came the interview, the special testing, and the scholarship offer. Had it all been a dream, like that awful season of *Dallas?*

While Torre stood slumped at the door, his heavy backpack already stuffed with the textbooks they'd been instructed to buy at Country Day's bookstore, Josie went back to the kitchen to search the front of the fridge for the school bus information form. She found it tucked under a Christmas tree-shaped magnet, peeking out from behind her town's September brush and leaf collection schedule. *If you have any questions*, the school form said, *please call Mrs. Irene Chapel.* Taking a deep breath, Josie dialed the number.

"Good morning, Country Day School," said the lilting voice on the other end of the line.

"Is this Mrs. Chapel?"

"*Sha-pelle*," corrected the voice. "How may I help you?" Josie thought she heard a hint of exasperation behind the studied cheeriness.

"Uh…oh…yes, well, this is Josie Messina? Torre's mom? He's starting seventh grade today?"

Ugh. Josie hated when she made every declarative sentence sound like a question. She did it whenever she felt insecure. Her ex-husband used to call it her "tell", the giveaway that belied her true state of mind.

"Oh my, yes, Mrs. Messina. I've just gotten off the phone with the bus driver. He told me he went up and down Sycamore Lane several times and couldn't find any house with the number fifty-five. I was just getting ready to phone you."

"Um, we're not on Sycamore Lane? We're on Sycamore Avenue?"

"Oh, oh goodness. Well, let me see. Now I can't quite picture that street. Is it behind the yacht club?

"Mrs. *Sha-pelle*," said Josie, hoping she put the emphasis on the proper syllable, "I can guess what the problem is. You're thinking of Little Fawn? But we're in Lower Fawn?"

"*Ohhhhh*, of course, Lower Fawn." Josie thought the transportation concierge put the emphasis on "Lower" the way one might intone that someone was carrying a *knock-off* Vuitton bag or driving a *pre-owned* Audi. She shrugged it off. Maybe she was just overly sensitive.

"Ah, no problem. Everyone gets the towns confused."

That wasn't exactly true. Other than the occasional rookie FedEx driver, few people ever got the glittering, upscale Little Fawn confused with its middle-class neighbor. Little Fawn, reput-

edly named for a Lenape Indian princess whose people inhab-
ited its Jersey shore peninsula long before it was taken over by
investment bankers, venture capitalists, and personal injury at-
torneys, was an enclave of venerable old estates and newly built
estate wannabes. Most of its homes, new and old, featured im-
peccable front lawns the size of football fields. Many had views
of the Intercoastal Waterway, and just about all had the kind of
swimming pools that were surrounded by "poolscapes" complete
with Belgian block walkways and teak lounge furniture straight
from Smith & Hawken.

Lower Fawn, just inland, had grown up in Little Fawn's
shadow, the princess's homely stepsister. In the early part of
the twentieth century, its inhabitants had been mostly ser-
vants who worked in the mansions to the east. For a while,
it morphed into a summer community, attracting an eclectic
mix of vacationing schoolteachers, young families hanker-
ing for an ocean view but settling for a whiff of sea breeze,
and—oddly enough—a cluster of vaudeville entertainers
whose touring burlesque company spent July and August at a
popular theatre "down the shore." From the 1950s on, Lower
Fawn had been staked out by an array of tradesmen whose
unofficial motto was, "If you can't be rich, live near the rich."
Landscapers, general contractors, plumbers, and electricians
all carved out niches for themselves by tending almost exclu-
sively to Little Fawn's house-proud gentry.

By the time the millennium rolled around, Lower Fawn itself
had become moderately gentrified, with some of the tradesmen
sprucing up their own modest ranch houses and split levels and
cashing out to new buyers: middle managers, IT engineers, and
the odd orthodontist still paying off dental school loans. Now,
the old-time tradesmen and the aspiring newcomers lived side
by side while keeping a wary distance. The first group fully realized that the second thought of Lower Fawn as a rest stop on the
turnpike to upward mobility.

But confuse the two towns? Who was kidding whom?

"Mrs. Messina, I am so sorry," Mrs. Chapel went on. "I see I
wrote the wrong town on the bus driver's itinerary. I must have

been on automatic pilot. You see, Torre is the only child coming from Lower Fawn this year."

The way she said it, Josie noted, you'd think that every other year Country Day had been inundated with boys and girls from her neck of the woods. But of course they were both aware that Torre's acceptance at the school had been a first for a Lower Fawn student.

"Silly me. *Mea culpa, mea maxima culpa,*" Mrs. Chapel exclaimed. "My bad."

Why the transportation concierge had seen fit to burst into Latin, let alone follow up with a hip-hop translation, Josie had no idea. But for the moment all she wanted to do was get her child off to his first day of school without any more delays.

"Again, I'm so very sorry," Mrs. Chapel said, "but it seems the bus driver had to continue on his route so that the other children wouldn't be late. I will most assuredly straighten it out by this afternoon, but for this morning...well, let me think. Is it possible we could send a taxi? Or, well, of course I suppose you're too busy to drop Torre off?"

Josie quickly weighed her options. The idea of putting her son in a cab all by himself was unthinkable; the poor boy was apprehensive enough as it was. Still, the timing was terrible. If she drove Torre, she'd miss half the breakfast rush at Cooler at the Shore. She'd have to stop downstairs and tell Pete and Jorge to run the grill and the cash register without her.

"It's not a problem," she heard herself say. "I'll bring him myself. I'll be there as soon as I can?"

Josie shook her head and sighed before composing her game face for Torre's benefit. Part of her was philosophical: Everyone made mistakes. These things happen, right? But another part of her, the part raised in a swath of New Jersey so rough and raw it made even her current surroundings seem like a five-star resort, got its hackles up.

"I know some more Latin," she mumbled under her breath. "*Itch-bay.*"

• • •

It was only a fifteen-minute drive to Little Fawn Country Day, but by the time Josie made the trip, sandwiched her van between the Beamers, and coaxed her offspring out of the passenger seat, it was apparent that school was already in session.

The rambling brick and stone main building—parts of it over a century old—emanated an aura of refined, studious quiet. Josie was conscious of her Payless sandals clacking irreverently on the marble floor of the lobby, which had once been the narthex of an Episcopal church. From her meetings at the school last spring, she knew Dr. Nobler's office was one flight up, and since she didn't know where any of Torre's classes were located she could think of no other option but to make her way to the headmaster.

The door to the headmaster's lushly appointed corner office was ajar. Josie knocked softly, peering around the thick slab of carved mahogany. Dr Nobler was talking with a reed-thin brunette who sported glasses with frames rimmed in rhinestones. Both were huddled over what appeared to be a large spreadsheet. The pair looked up at Josie and, much to her relief, Dr. Nobler broke into a beaming smile after an apparent moment of confusion. Practically jumping to his feet and scurrying around the desk, which couldn't have been easy for someone so rotund, he extended his chubby hand—not to Josie but to the boy standing behind her.

"Ah, Torre, Torre, Torre," he said. "There you are at last, young fellow. And how are you this very fine morning?"

"Uh, fine. Good. Um, and how are you, sir?"

Josie was, as always, impressed with her child. Unlike her, and most certainly unlike his long-vanished dad, Torre seemed to know what was called for in nearly any situation. As she had thousands of times before, she marveled at his maturity as well as his manners, not to mention his brains. How he ended up swimming out of the gene pool she and Sal and their peasant ancestors had created she never understood, but she knew this much: she would do everything she could to get him the education he deserved. This boy was going places—with or without a school bus.

"How am I doing?" echoed Dr. Nobler. "Couldn't be better! Thrilled to be kicking off a new school year. But, Torre, I must apologize to you and to your mom." He turned to face Josie.

"Mrs. Messina, I was just talking with Mrs. Chapel here. You know Mrs. Chapel, our transportation concierge and my chief administrative assistant? She was just explaining this morning's mix-up to me. We couldn't be more apologetic."

"That's right," agreed the thin woman, now on her feet as well. "We've got the entire bus route list here and we're sorting it all out. Torre will be dropped off this afternoon and picked up on time tomorrow morning. You can rest assured."

"Well, thanks so much," said Josie agreeably. "Thanks for straightening that all out. I…we were just wondering? Where is it that Torre is supposed to be right now?"

"Of course, of course," cooed Dr. Nobler. "Well, as it happens, I have a copy of Torre's schedule right here." He turned to Mrs. Chapel who quickly scanned his desk, spied a blue piece of paper poking out from beneath the base of a Tiffany lamp, and produced it with a flourish.

"There we go," he said. "Torre, as you know, yours is not going to be the typical seventh grade schedule. You'll have history and English and French with your peers but, as we've discussed, we've accelerated your math and science curriculum. You'll have these classes in our Upper School. Let's see, that's Advanced Trig/Precalculus, Honors Physics, and—say, guess what?"

Torre had no idea what. He'd known about the math and physics; after all, his aptitude in such subjects had landed him here. The truth was that no matter how much he'd rather have stayed in Lower Fawn Middle School with his friends, he'd been bored beyond tears in every math and science class offered there. Most of the teachers didn't take kindly to his ability to daydream so blatantly and still give the correct answers every time they roused him from his reveries. And after the Incident, Torre was completely in the doghouse as far as the faculty was concerned.

"I've managed to get you into our Computer Science Seminar with Mr. Jakes," Dr. Nobler went on. "It's seniors only—well, and now you, too. You'll love Mr. Jakes. He's our very own—what would you kids call it?—you know, super-geek! What do you say to that, young man?"

"Cool," Torre answered. "I mean great. That's neat."

He didn't really relish the idea of being in a class with kids five years older than he was. He couldn't imagine how they would react to the presence of a twelve-year-old twerp. But computers—all right! Computers were one of his obsessions. With the tips he earned helping his mom make deliveries, he'd bought an old Dell laptop on eBay and souped it up to the point where his mother swore it could do everything but the laundry. She'd confiscated it after the Incident, but she'd relented over the summer. Now computers would be part of his schoolwork. How could she complain?

Watching Torre's cherubic face brighten, Josie smiled. Things were looking up.

"Mrs. Chapel," Dr Nobler said, "why don't you escort Torre to Room 216 for his math class?"

The transportation concierge, looking only slightly taken aback when asked to provide guided transportation, offered a close-lipped smile as she motioned for Torre to follow her. For a moment both Josie and Dr. Nobler stood silently, staring at the backs of the two as they walked briskly out into the corridor. To Josie's immense relief, Torre turned briefly to give her a small farewell wave. She beamed at the boy as if he were the answer to her every prayer, and although she did not notice, Dr. Nobler did the same.

Josie looked at her watch. She had to get out of there if she was going to get the lunchtime soup special going. She hoped Dr. Nobler wouldn't go on and on. In their few encounters so far, she'd noticed how much he liked to talk about Country Day, its venerable traditions, and the grand plans he had for its future. Luckily, at that moment three women swept through the door in a whirl of chatter and laughter.

"We're *heeere*," announced a tall, broad brunette dressed in a short-sleeved, lace-trimmed shift printed in a cornucopia of Easter egg pastels. Blinking emphatically, she registered the presence of a stranger in their midst.

"Oh, sorry, Dr. Nobler," she said. "Are we interrupting? We thought it was time for the Mothers' Welcome Tea meeting."

"Not at all, Lydia," said the headmaster, beckoning her and the rest of the trio toward him. "Right on time. Splendid! Oh, by the way, I'd like you all to meet Mrs. Messina. Her boy is starting seventh grade here today. She'll be one of the newcomers we're welcoming!"

Josie smiled, tugging at the hem of her button-down shirt and willing her five-foot-two frame to stand at its most erect.

"Mrs. Messina, I'd like you meet our hospitality committee. This is Lydia Thorn," he said, gesturing to the Easter egg lady. Lydia peered down at Josie from what was, between her natural height and her bright pink wedge sandals, a good ten-inch advantage, and perfunctorily raised the corners of her mouth.

"And this is Celeste Battin." He nodded toward a platinum blonde dressed in tennis whites. Josie recognized her, but Celeste's blank stare and brief greeting indicated no such reciprocity.

Josie knew that Celeste Battin was not the sort of woman who paid attention to anyone who served her from behind a deli counter, not even if the server was also the proprietor. Josie, on the other hand, was a keen observer of her customers. She'd never known Celeste's name, but she knew her standard order: a quarter of a pound of seafood salad and one turkey meatball. South Beach diet fare if she ever saw it. As far as Josie knew, Celeste hadn't eaten a carbohydrate since 2006. The sporty blonde hadn't stopped in at Cooler at the Shore for a while though, and today Josie noted something different about her appearance. Over the course of the summer, Celeste's cup size seemed to have increased from a B to a D. Josie never forgot a face, or a figure.

"And this is Emily Luffhauser," Dr. Nobler went on. Josie thought she noted a hint of genuflection as he turned to the oldest and most regal member of the hospitality ladies. Josie knew who Emily Luffhauser was as well, but that was to be expected. Everyone in the Fawns knew the ubiquitous Luffhauser clan. Emily and her husband Brad had five children, and Brad's two brothers and their wives had six children apiece. The extended family occupied three adjacent estates on Little Fawn's Luffhauser Lane, which wound up a hillside that overlooked the Intercoastal and afforded vistas of the ocean beyond.

The Luffhausers had settled in the area sometime in the late 1600s and made their fortunes in banking and agriculture, when New Jersey was truly the garden state. Today the Luffhauser name adorned half the public and private enterprises in the area, or so it seemed. There was Luffhauser Fields, donated to the community as a nature preserve; Luffhauser Trust, the local savings and loan; and Luffhauser Farms, a sprawling array of orchards surrounding a vast plant and tree nursery. The Farms complex included a gourmet market that had evolved from a roadside tomato stand into a destination so popular that even Manhattan foodies flocked to it by the busload on autumn Saturdays to buy fresh spiced apple cider and voluminous pumpkin pies. Somehow, some way, everyone seemed tethered to the Luffhausers by fewer than three degrees of separation. Even Josie's dog had come from the Luffhauser Adoption Wing at the local SPCA.

Clad in a knee-length khaki pencil skirt and an olive cardigan that set off her creamy skin and auburn hair, Emily smiled graciously at Josie and extended her hand.

"How very nice to meet you," she said warmly, the way the Queen of England might speak to a six-year-old who brought a bouquet of daisies to the palace gate.

Stifling the urge to curtsey, Josie murmured, "Likewise?"

"Perhaps you'd like to stay and help plan our little get-together?" Dr. Nobler asked Josie. But the almost imperceptible shake of his head as he said it was just one of the many reasons Josie mumbled apologies about running late. She exited before anyone could think of a reason to dissuade her.

As she made her way across the parking lot, her feelings of awkwardness receded. She had other things to think about, like her lunchtime special soup. Torre was safely delivered, Dr. Nobler had been unable to rhapsodize at length about the charms of his school, and at last she could focus on her White Bean and Broccoli—or so she thought, until she heard that voice. *That voice!* She'd know it anywhere; who wouldn't?

"*Jo-Jo.* Josephine Messina. Holy cow, is that you?"

It was the unmistakable voice of Billy Stand; that sandy, seductive growl had mesmerized the iconic rock star's millions of diehard fans for nearly two decades. Like virtually everyone else of her generation—and Torre's generation, too—Josie knew the words to Billy Stand's every stadium-packing anthem and heart-rending ballad. But all she could think of as he called her name was how much his voice had changed since the days when she knew him as a kid in Wild Bay, New Jersey—a kid she babysat for years. Little Billy Stankiewicz.

"Billy?" she said. "Well, hi, I…hi! Oh my God, *Billy*. What are you doing here?"

On stage, the sight of Billy Stand routinely made female fans from age sixteen to sixty fight back the urge to fling their underpants at him—with a few losing the fight and flinging away. But right now the sight of him wearing a pair of gym shorts, running shoes, a sweaty T-shirt, and his trade-mark headband left Josie as stunned as if she'd encountered a pointy-headed space alien. Billy had left Wild Bay behind when he was seventeen, nearly twenty years ago, yet here he was right in front of her.

"My twins start kindergarten today. Forgot their snacks." He smiled, brandishing two brown paper bags marked *Lucy* and *Harry*.

"I thought—I mean, I figured you were still living in California?"

"Just moved back. Bought a place down the road. What about you? You teaching here, Teach?"

"Teach" was Billy's old nickname for her, an homage to all the nights Josie had spent attempting to help Little Billy do his homework and study for his spelling tests when all he'd wanted to do was blast records and make up melodies on his harmonica. Catchy melodies, even then.

"You know," he added, "I never would have made it as far as eleventh grade if it hadn't been for you." He'd never made it any further, but as high school dropouts go, he was quite possibly America's most successful.

Somehow Billy's calling her by the long-ago sobriquet calmed Josie down. "No, I'm not teaching. My kid goes here, too—starting today. He's twelve."

"No kidding! Hey, that's awesome. We're gonna have to catch up, you and me." He grinned and opened his arms. "*Teach.*"

With that, he gathered his old friend up into a bear hug, lifted her off the ground, and twirled her full circle. All Josie's self-consciousness, along with any thoughts of her awaiting Soup of the Day, dissolved as she and Billy let out a simultaneous whoop of laughter.

And in that moment—as Lydia, blinking; Celeste, frowning; and Emily, scratching her head—looked on from the bay window of Dr. Nobler's office, Josephine Messina instantly gained herself three relentless new best friends.

• • •

Language Arts Journal, September 17
Torre Messina

After two weeks of writing these English journals I believe Mrs. Tripper really means it when she says they are private. She never looks at them at all. She just looks up once in a while to make sure we're writing during journal time. Sometimes she reminds us to underline <u>feeling words</u>. Reading time is the same. Mrs. T. just looks up once in a while to make sure we're actually reading and not listening to iPods or something.

Mrs. T. says Country Day is lucky to be part of OLA (that's our Organic Language Arts program) because we're not going to get turned off to English by being forced to memorize grammar rules or read stuff we don't like. <u>I feel OLA rocks</u> because now I can finish the "Dune" series, which is amazing. And then I'm going to read "Stranger in a Strange Land" by Robert Heinlein, which my friend Josh told me was great. And then I'll reread all the "Lord of the Rings" books, which are even better than the movies.

Not all the kids read books though. Mindy Battin sits next to me and she is reading a Rolling Stone article on Lady Gaga. Mindy says she wants to be a rock singer. She talks about it all the time. <u>I feel that Mindy is annoying</u>, but whatever.

In the mornings I have Upper School classes. I definitely <u>felt weird</u> in those the first few days. Some of the kids there looked at me the way my mom looks at her tuna salad when she thinks it might be turning. But after a couple of days they were pretty nice to me. When Persephone Thorn found out I was really good at math she was extra nice, even though she's a senior. She said if I helped her study for the SATs she'd give me her old Xbox. But I told her I'd help her for free, because she seems awfully nervous about getting a better score this time. Besides Mom says no Xbox. (I feel that is really not fair.)

Mom seems pretty happy though, so maybe I can work on her. She told me she ran into an old friend here and guess who it turned out to be? Billy Stand! He came by our deli, Cooler at the Shore, the other day and I never heard Mom laugh so hard. She said they talked about old times. I felt shy to talk to Billy, but he seemed like a really nice guy.

I miss my friends from Lower Fawn Middle School – especially Josh. But basically I feel things are going okay. The best thing is the computer seminar. I am learning all kinds of stuff about Unix from Mr. Jakes. Even more than I knew before. Mr. J says I have aptitude. That's sure different than the way they put it back at Lower Fawn Middle School.

But I don't want to write about that whole Incident. I feel tired of writing anyway.

I feel hungry.

CHAPTER 2:

Mothers' Welcome Tea

September 20
FROM: Dr. Preston Nobler
TO: All Faculty and Administrative Staff
RE: Mothers' Welcome Tea

As you all know, this afternoon is our Mothers' Welcome Tea. As always, I know we will do all we can to show our appreciation to LFCD moms, both new and seasoned. As you no doubt are aware, this year's tea will be a very special event, as I will be revealing our building plan and Capital Campaign.

I know you are as excited as I am about our plans for expansion, and I am confident you will convey your unbridled enthusiasm to our mothers so that they may feel inspired—and in turn inspire others—to embrace our fundraising theme: _Givers of Knowledge (GOK)._

It is, of course, our devoted mothers who will determine our ultimate success. As the old saying goes, "Man may be head of the family, but woman is the neck that turns the head."

The headmaster sighed with satisfaction as he pressed "Send," distributing his Mothers' Welcome Tea missive far and wide. He was particularly proud of the last line of his memo, which the Fates had seen fit to transmit to him via a fortune cookie only the night before. He sat back in his reclining swivel chair, adjusted its lumbar support, and allowed himself the luxury of planting his feet on his desk blotter. He admired his freshly shined Gucci loafers, bought especially for today's occasion because, as anyone knew, you had to look like money when you asked for money.

Today, Nobler was an optimistic man. After a downhill slump, things seemed at last to be turning his way. In the previous school year enrollment was down, and then there was that dicey business with Miss Markle, the kindergarten teacher. But as of this fall, his school had a rock star parent *and* that little math genius. And, thanks to the impact of the lingering economic downturn on the owner of the school's immediately neighboring estate—a hedge funder whose Icelandic mortgage assets were now "frozen," as Nobler liked to quip—Country Day had been able to obtain adjacent acreage for a fraction of its worth at foreclosure.

At last, the headmaster could proceed with his dream of adding onto the school: a bigger gymnasium; a new technology and media hub; a performing arts center; and most important of all, a classroom annex that, among other things, would allow him to initiate both a Pre-K and a Pre-Pre-K grade. Now, students could enter Country Day at age three and stay through high school. Fifteen years of knowledge! Fifteen years of tradition! Fifteen years of tuition!

Best of all, his bold new plans would stem the tide of defecting parents. In still relatively small but escalating numbers, some malcontents were swooping up their progeny from his hallowed halls and depositing the kids—along with some hefty tuition checks—across town at OLPS, Our Lady of Perpetual Sorrows, LFCD's perennial rival school. But who would want to leave now, what with all the marvelous buzz, all the excitement, and all the opportunities?

Besides, he would have the added advantage of a two-year jumpstart on OLPS. Once he could enroll Little Fawn's three-year-olds in Pre-Pre-K, he'd have the Country Day school spirit imprinted on their malleable marshmallow brains while they were still learning how to pee. Even if the OLPS kids kept scoring higher on those damned new statewide standardized tests for private education, his school would come out ahead. Anyway, he thought, his smile reflecting in his shoes, the New Jersey Annual Scholastic Survey wasn't going to be a problem anymore. LFCD was about to kick NJ ASS.

• • •

Sitting at her vanity lit by a rectangle of pink-tinted incandescent bulbs, Celeste Battin smiled—or at least she practiced smiling. It was a chore. For one thing, the Botox had kicked in; for another, she really didn't feel like smiling. Nevertheless, she had to put a good face on things. She'd hidden the whole sordid Marisa Markle business from her friends this long; she wasn't going to crack now.

Staring past her image in the mirror, Celeste spied a reflected photo of Andy and their kids, Mindy and little Lars, all soaked head-to-toe from a dolphin hug at Disney's Discovery Cove. The picture had been snapped at a happier time—a time before her husband had taken up with Lars's kindergarten teacher. She never blamed him so much as her. After all, Andy had scored his tens of millions years ago, cashing out of his dot-com start-up just before the bubble popped and splattered his former partners with worthless stock options. He'd been just over forty years old with time on his hands when the affair began. But that Markle woman—if she'd plotted out her lesson plans as carefully as she'd plotted her campaign to snag someone else's husband, maybe Lars would have entered first grade able to read, like all those OLPS kids.

Well, never mind. She and Andy had agreed to put it all behind them. She wasn't sure exactly what footing they were on, but she knew for a fact he wouldn't be dipping into Marisa Markle's cookie jar anymore. Her husband's new tech start-up kept him busy and away in Mumbai or Singapore for months at a stretch. She was grateful for one thing: at least none of the other mothers knew about what had gone on. That was why she insisted to Dr. Nobler that Miss Markle had to stay. If he had fired the little tramp there might have been talk. Besides, as long as Markle stayed, Celeste could keep an eye on her.

This afternoon would certainly bring a Markle sighting. Best to keep a distance, Celeste instructed herself. Besides, she had someone else she wanted to talk with at the tea: that Josie person, the one who hugged Billy Stand. What was her story? Mindy, Celeste's seventh grader, wanted nothing more than to meet the rock legend. Well, meet him and sing for him. Ever since she found out her idol had moved back from California and settled in their town, Mindy talked of practically nothing else, which was extremely trying because the girl talked all the time.

Celeste noticed that one of her pink light bulbs had burned out. She pulled a replacement from the stash in her dresser. She hoarded the complexion-flattering 60-watt babies as insurance against the dreaded day when the global warming Nazis would make everyone switch to those unholy compact fluorescents.

She pulled on a bosom-hugging, cream-colored sweater. Her new D-cups stood so proudly at attention that she felt like saluting. She practiced smiling again, and then walked to the kitchen to peel a hard-boiled egg. No matter what happened, she wasn't going to let herself be tempted by the carb-loaded tea snacks that were lying in wait. She'd read that Kate Moss had a diet mantra: "Nothing tastes as good as skinny feels." In her head, Celeste recited her own motto: "Gloat. Don't bloat."

· · ·

Lydia Thorn inserted her contact lenses, deposited some eye drops onto her perennially dry and scratchy corneas, and blinked. She surveyed her walk-in closet, which was overwhelmingly stocked with Lilly Pulitzer designs. Long ago she had decided that her trademark look would be colorful, casual elegance, and once Lydia latched onto a winning formula she was loath to let it go.

She picked out a lime green crew neck T-shirt, a long-sleeved, hip length, pale rose cardigan with just a hint of flounce at the neckline, and a pair of print capris. Perfect as always, she assessed, never dreaming that some might have questioned the wisdom of the hip accentuation.

Thus inspired, Lydia used the few minutes she had left before she had to leave for the Mothers' Welcome Tea to visit her favorite designer's website and see what Lilly had in store for the holiday season. Before she could help it, she clicked on the link to Pulitzer's famed sorority scarves emblazoned with Greek insignia. Lydia longed for the day when her daughter Persephone would order a supply. Of course there were only two sororities at Brown, her own alma mater, and Lydia herself had been snubbed by both of them. She shuddered at the bitter memory, and then shrugged it off. The ever-popular Persey was sure to pledge. In any case, she could wait to worry about that once Persey got into Brown—if she got in.

Oh no, no, no. Don't go there, Lydia warned herself. She didn't like to think about the blood sport that college admissions had become because it gave her frown lines. These days, even being a legacy didn't guarantee a thing, although she still hoped it would afford her girl the tiniest edge. On the bright side, Persephone's grades at Country Day were pretty good overall—Lydia would expect nothing less for the tuition she paid. And soon, Lydia would make it her business to remind the teachers who would be writing her daughter's recommendations of all Persey's outstanding achievements: Co-under-captain of Girl's Lacrosse, assistant choreographer of the cheerleader squad, official videographer of last summer's Little Fawn Youth Group Mission to Rebuild—what was it?—Something-or-Other in Haiti.

But of course, a lot was riding on the October SATs. This was Persey's last chance to bring up her mediocre math score before sending in her Early Decision application. Lydia recalled Persephone saying that the school's new seventh grade math whiz was helping her during study hall, of all things. Still, she'd be sure to thank the boy's mother this afternoon. As a former psych major at Brown, Lydia knew the value of positive reinforcement.

• • •

Emily Luffhauser looked over the list of delicacies she was having sent from Luffhauser Farms to Little Fawn Country Day's tea. There were eight blueberry pies; four peach pies; four strawberry-rhubarb pies; six dozen raisin-pecan scones; eight dozen chocolate chunk cookies; twenty-four gallons of apple cider; three large cheese, crudité, and cracker plates; and enough mini-quiche to pave the new courtyard on Dr. Nobler's drawing board. Oh yes, she knew about the Capital Campaign. The Luffhausers knew just about everything that went on in Little Fawn. You could hardly apply for a permit to re-plumb a bathroom, let alone concoct a twenty-one million dollar school expansion plan, without requiring the signature of some civic-minded Luffhauser serving their requisite stint on town council.

Emily totaled up the cost of today's donated food. It was enough to stock the Friends of Wild Bay Food Bank, one of her pet projects, for two weeks. Now *that* was a worthy cause. Nobler, on the other hand, just didn't know when to stop asking for things. She knew she and her husband Brad would be hit up big-time for the building campaign, and they were weary of shelling out. It would be one thing if they were certain their five children were getting a first-class education, but in the past few years she had become less sure. The headmaster paid lip service to tradition, but where academics were concerned he embraced the kind of trendy notions that had transformed America's youth into a cadre of dunces. Organic Language Arts indeed, she sniffed.

Last year, one of Emily's sisters-in-law had pulled her two youngest children from Country Day and transferred them to Our Lady of Perpetual Sorrows. Everyone was aware that OLPS students had scored significantly higher than LFCD students on New Jersey's Annual Scholastic Survey for two years running. Maybe she should think about OLPS for her brood as well.

Emily looked at the bottom line for today's tab once more and grimaced. Why couldn't someone else cater for a change? What about that Josie person?

• • •

Josie was only lukewarm about attending the Mothers' Welcome
Tea. She liked being home when Torre got off the bus. Today her
son would have only Newton to share an after-school hug. What's
more, she couldn't figure out what to wear. She ended up defaulting to the New York/New Jersey "can't go wrong" standard: black
slacks, black top, and understated sterling jewelry. Truthfully, she
never thought she looked all that great in black. It made her
petite frame seem even tinier and her fair skin even paler.

Despite having spent every one of her forty-two summers at
the Jersey shore, Josie usually steered clear of the beach from
May to August. Regardless of her southern Italian background,
she burned to a crisp in the sun. Her family always said she took
after Grandpa Frank, who'd sat in a bathtub full of vinegar to
soothe the burns he invariably got on beach trips to Coney Island.
She barely remembered her grandfather, but in family photos
he looked more like a Swede than a Sicilian. It sort of made
sense; during the course of history everyone and his brother had
invaded Sicily. Like Newton, she was a mutt.

Josie was also reluctant to attend the afternoon's event
because she simply couldn't imagine herself mingling with the
other Country Day mothers. She couldn't think what she would
talk about, but as it turned out, the ambience at the Mothers'
Welcome Tea was nothing if not welcoming.

As soon as she walked through the door of the school's library,
where the festivities were taking place, Emily targeted Josie with
the speed and accuracy of a Scud missile, flying across the room
to greet her with a warm double-clasp handshake. Emily com-
mandeered her catch toward a far corner where Celeste and
Lydia, already huddled in conversation, were pointedly ignoring
a vast pastry platter beside them.

"Well, Josie. It is Josie, isn't it? Here you are at last," said Emily.
"I confess we've all just been shamelessly gossiping about you."
She believed in employing truth whenever possible in order to
charm and disarm.

"Oh? You have?"

"Indeed. You remember Celeste and Lydia? We all met in Dr. Nobler's office. And I'm Emily, of course."

"Oh yes. Of course."

"Well, Lydia was just complimenting your son. What an admirable young man! Did you know he was helping Lydia's daughter prepare for her math SATs? And to think he's twelve!"

"He is? I mean, yes he *is* twelve. But, er, no, I didn't know he was helping...uh..."

"Persephone," said Lydia.

"*Persephone?*"

"Her friends call her Persey."

"Oh. That makes...I see. Well," said Josie, wondering why Torre never mentioned anything about it. "He's always looking for an excuse to do more math."

"Amazing," said Emily. "This school needs more like him."

"You know," Celeste chimed in, "I think my daughter Mindy has English class with your son."

"Oh yes?" said Josie. She hadn't realized Torre had made such a big impression. "How nice."

"Is Torre enjoying Country Day?" Emily asked earnestly.

"Well, yes! Yes, he is. You know it's a bit of an adjustment and all, but he's doing pretty well."

"Well, we're lucky to have him—and to have you." said Lydia. "Now tell me," she added, as if they hadn't already been nosing around trying to find out everything they could about the Messinas, "where did Torre used to go to school?"

"Um...Lower Fawn Elementary and Lower Fawn Middle School?" *Stop talking in questions,* Josie scolded herself. *You're just having a friendly conversation.*

"Well, their loss is our gain," said Celeste, forcing herself to maintain eye contact with Josie despite the fact that her peripheral vision had just registered Marisa Markle entering the room.

"And are you from Lower Fawn originally?" asked Emily.

"Why no, no. Actually I grew up in Wild Bay."

Wild Bay! Now that was something Emily hadn't already discovered on her own. That must explain Josie's connection to Billy Stand. But wait—this was getting even more interesting.

Emily put two and two together and, unlike the math challenged Persephone Thorn, came up with four. Now she had even more reason to keep talking to Josie, and she decided to double down on her efforts.

"You don't say," she exclaimed. "Well, it just so happens I'm involved in a bit of a project down in Wild Bay. I'd love to tell you about it. By the way, can I get you a raisin-pecan scone?"

Josie didn't care for raisins, the texture of which set her teeth on edge, but she certainly didn't want to risk upending such a convivial moment. This event was going better than she'd expected. She nibbled the concoction out of politeness, avoiding the dried-up, wrinkled grapes as best she could. Emily, Lydia, and Celeste (who, Josie thought, seemed just a little quieter than the others) included her in a dizzying splash of Country Day mother talk. Their animated discourse spanned everything from charitable causes to upcoming social events to the newly released *U.S. News and World Report* college rankings to the dubious wardrobe choices of other mothers standing just out of earshot.

No one asked about Billy Stand, of course. Josie's new friends would never have been so crass as to seem curious about a celebrity. After all, Country Day had had its share of famous parents over the years. There was that Asian newscaster whose family left after she took a job with CNN in London (a shame, they'd all agreed, since Asians invariably brought up school-wide test averages, what with those psycho tiger mothers and all). And there was that state senator who pulled his kids out just before his bribery and extortion trial. Yes, they were used to mingling with all kinds.

Besides, there would be plenty of time to draw Josie out as the school year unfolded. If any of them secretly wished that if they kept her chatting long enough she just might reveal a morsel of juicy information about Billy, their swelling balloons of hope were about to be popped by Preston Nobler.

The headmaster had stepped behind a podium set up in the center of the library and begun dramatically clearing his throat in a ritual that all the veteran Country Day mothers knew could mean only one thing.

"Here goes the Bloviator," Emily whispered.

"Good afternoon, ladies," he trilled. In his chinos, white Oxford shirt, and blue blazer, Nobler looked like a puffier, balder version of his young male charges, but for the fact that his tie was emblazoned with the Little Fawn Country Day crest, which displayed a wise-looking owl hovering on a branch above a somewhat startled looking baby deer. The tie was part of the LFCD wearables line, which, although prominently displayed in the bookshop, had never caught on with the student body. The parents had more than made up for this, though, by snatching up adult-sized sweatshirts, ball caps, and rain ponchos.

"I can tell from the level of noise in the room that all of you are as delighted as I am to see one another after the summer. Since I don't see a single wallflower among you, I know that all of our new mothers have been embraced by you 'old' mothers. Ha-ha!" He grinned at his own word choice in a way he hoped was impish. "That is, I mean to say, mothers already in the Country Day family." He paused for the anticipated tinkle of laughter, clearing his throat when it failed to materialize.

"We have many events coming up at which you can all get to know one another better. Mrs. Chapel has 'Save the Date' handouts, so please make sure you get one before you leave.

"And now," he continued, "I have some very exciting news to share." Stepping out from behind the podium, he walked over to one of the library tables. After several moments of preliminary hand waving, as if he were a magician about to conjure a bunny or a bouquet of daisies out of thin air, he pulled aside the tablecloth covering a large anonymous lump. What he revealed was not another tray of tea treats, as some might have hoped (or dreaded), but rather a glass-sheathed model of the new and improved Little Fawn Country Day campus.

He launched into a description of his elaborate vision, using phrases such as "cutting edge technology," "art studios," "performance space," "refurbished college counseling offices," "expanded athletic fields," and "a 16,000 square-foot early childhood facility to attract the best and brightest young learners in our community." Mothers around the room smiled and cooed, each of them more determined than the next to mask the thought uppermost in her mind: *How much is this going to cost me?* But when the headmaster asked Mrs. Chapel to dim the lights and segued into a lengthy PowerPoint charting the particulars of groundbreaking dates, construction phases, and traffic rerouting plans, the attention of some began to wander.

Celeste glanced repeatedly at the raven-haired Marisa Markle, kindergarten adventuress. Dressed in a Jezebel-red wrap dress, she stood next to the refreshments and grazed on chocolate chip cookies the way only the very young and naturally lithe could do.

Then Celeste noticed something odd. It seemed that some of the other mothers were also glancing at Miss Markle, and then at Celeste, and then at Miss Markle again.

"*Son of a bitch,*" she murmured. She aimed a look at the headmaster that would have earned her life without parole if looks could kill. Nobler had to be the source of the gossip that had evidently been circulating. *That miserable weasel never knows when to shut up.*

As Dr. Nobler gushed on about donor opportunities, personalized pavers, and plaques engraved with the names of generous givers, Josie reassured herself that no one could expect her, the single working mother of a scholarship student, to contribute to this lavish scheme. She began to survey the room as well, but her eyes didn't veer anywhere near the notorious Miss Markle, of whom she knew nothing special. Instead she rested her gaze at the far corner of the library, where another woman stood behind a large potted fern in a nook beside the entryway. The woman, dressed simply in jeans and a dark gray T-shirt, sported sunglasses and a floppy, wide-brimmed straw hat. She looked almost like a caricature of someone incognito. But Josie, who'd known her long ago, still recognized the freckled porcelain doll face and the unmistakable strawberry blonde hair of Billy's hometown bride, MaryAnn Stand.

Although Josie had never known MaryAnn very well, she wanted to say hello, and gently tried to extricate herself from her circle of companions. But it was just then that Nobler concluded his presentation to the sound of polite applause. Even before

Mrs. Chapel flicked on the rows of overheard lights, would-be Givers of Knowledge were gravitating en masse toward the comfort of more refreshments. By the time Josie was able to stand on tiptoe and peer through the herd, the nook behind the potted fern was empty.

The afternoon wound to a close, and with so much excitement in the air—so many opinions, questions, and appraisals; so many sugary snacks; and so many equally sugarcoated congratulations offered up to the headmaster—a few minor details went unnoticed. No one noticed when Celeste surreptitiously slipped one blueberry scone, and then another, into her Longchamps tote. And certainly no one noticed that MaryAnn Stand, who had stayed but a minute and spoken to no one, found her way into the faculty lounge ladies room, pulled a miniature bottle of Courvoisier out of her handbag, and took a long swig.

• • •

Language Arts Journal, October 4 Torre Messina

This past Saturday my friend Josh and I got to help out at the deli again because Jorge couldn't come in. And Billy Stand came back! Billy said he can't get enough of Mom's tuna salad. Which <u>I totally feel I agree with him about</u>. This time Billy brought his twins. The boy and the girl both have this kind of pinkish blonde hair that Mom said is their mother's hair. And Billy Stand, who I guess knew my dad a little, said I had Sal's wild hair. So that was amazing.

Anyway, Josh and I took the twins back into the kitchen while Billy talked to mom. We let Lucy and Harry dip hunks of bread into the big pot of tomato sauce. Hunks of bread dipped in that sauce was my favorite thing to eat when I was their age. They thought it was great too.

When we brought the twins back out they had tomato sauce beards. Billy Stand thought that was hilarious.

<u>I feel like I miss my Dad.</u>

CHAPTER 3:

Spaghetti Night

Bring Your Appetite to Spaghetti Night!

*The Little Fawn Country Day Hospitality Committee
and Dr. Preston Nobler*

*invite you to
a fun, fun, fundraiser!
Please join us for an*

All-You-Can-Eat Evening

*In the LFCD Dining Hall on Saturday, October 15
7:30 p.m.*

*Tickets: $100 per person
Gift Basket Auction!
All proceeds to benefit the
Givers of Knowledge Capital Campaign*

Dress: Elegant Casual

In the Cooler at the Shore kitchen, Josie hunkered over an eight-gallon stainless steel stockpot. She frowned. This particular batch of spaghetti sauce seemed a little off. It wasn't the tomatoes; they were Luffhauser Farms' best, courtesy of Emily. Contributing the produce was the least she could do, Emily had insisted, after coaxing Josie into catering the Country Day Spaghetti Night fundraiser.

"Coaxing" wasn't exactly the word Josie would have used. Actually, she'd felt a bit strong-armed by Emily's sudden brainstorm that Cooler was the "obvious" choice to donate the food for the first of the Givers of Knowledge festivities—one where parents, teachers, and students paid handsomely for bottomless plates of pasta and salad. Her first panicked thought was that donating all this fare would cost her a small fortune, but she also saw it as a better alternative than coughing up a check. Ever practical, Josie hoped that this sort of exposure would earn her many potential new catering customers among the Little Fawn crowd. Tonight could be an investment in the future, and in Torre's college fund, so it was especially important that all go well.

She reached over to the counter for more of her secret ingredient: kosher salt. "Jewish salt," her mother used to call it. "Blessed by a rabbi—or, well, I don't know what they do to make it so good, but it makes everything taste better," she'd mumble as she poured it liberally into the Sunday "gravy," which was what first generation Italian-Americans like her mother called tomato sauce. She'd never understood why.

Josie's mother Rose, rest her soul, hadn't imparted very many culinary secrets to her only daughter. Although she never abandoned her Sunday gravy ritual, all the other days of the week Rose was only too happy to bow to New World culinary conveniences that minimized her stove time. Over the course of Josie's childhood, Rose became an enthusiastic early adopter of Swanson frozen dinners, Hamburger Helper, Shake 'n Bake, and Sara Lee (a prodigious amount of which was found in her grocery cart when she succumbed to a fatal heart attack at the A&P). The rest of Josie's recipes were, for the most part, dreamed up by her ex-husband, who had a knack for putting a flavorful contemporary spin on dishes handed down to him by his Neapolitan forebears. Sal at least had the decency to write the recipes down before cleaning out their joint savings account and vanishing ten years ago.

Other than following his recipes, Josie tried hard not to think about Sal. On her runs to PetSmart for Newton's favorite dog food, she often drove more than a mile out of her way just to avoid going by Monmouth Raceway, the venue where Sal would routinely blow their business's weekly profit—and then some. She'd done everything she could to get her husband to stop gambling and to get him some help. But she knew it was futile when she'd told Sal that gambling was a disease and he had replied, "How much do you want to bet?"

It did no good to be resentful, Josie reminded herself. Sal had left her with a small mountain of bills and two mortgages on the building that housed Cooler at the Shore and the apartment above it—a place the couple had told themselves they would inhabit only for a short time while their business got off the ground. But he did leave the recipes: the Lemon Wine Sauce Linguini, the Devil Hot Shrimp Scampi, the Turkey Drumstick Parmigiana, and others that had drawn a loyal clientele over the years.

And of course he'd given her Torre. Things happened the way they were supposed to, she believed. It was the most philosophy for which she'd ever had time.

Josie salted and stirred until she heard the string of bells on the front door that announced a customer's arrival. Peering out from the kitchen she saw Celeste, once again clad in tennis whites, accompanied by an adolescent girl carrying a guitar case.

"Hey Pete, I'll get it," Josie told her young counterman. "Can you keep an eye on things in the kitchen?"

Pete, whose eyes had instantly glued to Celeste's double Ds, gave Josie a mournful glance as he edged past her.

"Celeste," said Josie. "How nice to see you. And is this your daughter?"

"Yes, this is my Mindy." Celeste beamed. "Fresh from Saturday morning guitar lessons. She's learning to accompany herself when she sings."

"Really! Well, good to meet you, Mindy. I have to say I admire anyone who can play the guitar."

Josie saw Celeste and her daughter exchange a glance, but couldn't imagine why. "She's really talented," Celeste volunteered. "*Really*. It's like she's attached to that thing."

But Mindy had already leaned her guitar case along the glass display front of the deli counter and begun to appraise the contents of the case's many food trays.

"Well, she's attached except when there's something good to eat, that is," Celeste corrected. "You know, Josie, it's such a coincidence that you own this place. I used to come in here all the time for—"

"Seafood salad and turkey meatballs," Josie finished the sentence for her.

"Yes! Yes, that's right. What a memory you have. I wish I—"

"Hey," Mindy interrupted, apparently having found what she hunted. "This tuna—is this the stuff Billy Stand comes in for?"

Momentarily taken aback, Josie wondered how Mindy could have known that Billy Stand had taken to frequenting her establishment. Well, that kind of thing got around, she supposed. Maybe that was why business had been brisker than usual lately. But how did the girl know Billy liked her tuna salad? Josie shrugged it off, assuming Torre must have mentioned it. Little Mindy, in her cut-offs and peasant blouse, looked like the kind of girl a pubescent boy might want to impress.

"The tuna's made with olive oil, red peppers, and onions. A lot of people like it. Want to try some?" She spooned a bit of the mixture onto a small paper plate and handed Mindy a plastic fork.

"*Mmmppff*. Good," said Mindy between bites. "*Mppff elppff mumph* Billy like?"

"Don't talk with your mouth full," said Celeste.

"What's Billy like?" deciphered Josie. "Well, he's a really nice guy. Always was."

"I said what *else* does he *like*? I meant what *food*," Mindy clarified. But Celeste spotted the opening her daughter had inadvertently created and dived immediately into it, head over heels.

"What? You know Billy Stand well? How amazing! I had no idea. Gosh, you must have some wonderful stories to tell."

"Yeah, what's the dirt?" Mindy chimed in, licking her fingers.

Josie smiled. She guessed she did have some pretty good stories to tell. Billy had been a sweet kid, but filled with a kind of manic energy that probably would have earned him a full-fledged ADHD diagnosis and an Adderall prescription today. He was the wild boy from Wild Bay.

The Stankiewiczs had moved next door to Josie and her parents the summer when Billy was two and Josie was seven. The first few times she saw him, he was tearing around his backyard pulling off all his clothes and shrieking with glee as he darted under the lawn sprinkler. Well, she certainly wasn't going to plant that image in Mindy's head.

"Well, wow. Let me think," she said, searching her memory for some small and safe nugget of biographical trivia to sate the girl's—and her mother's—curiosity. "I tried to help him with homework sometimes. He wasn't a great speller."

"Spelling's a silly convention," Mindy opined. "It's not organic. That's what Mrs. Tripper says."

"Oh? It is?" said Josie. Huh. School certainly had a different twist on it in Little Fawn.

Celeste rolled her eyes. "Don't get me started," she said to her daughter, but the thirteen-year-old girl made it clear she wasn't interested in debating the finer points of language arts instruction.

"So what else does Billy like to eat?" she repeated.

"Those," Josie said, pointing to an item in the dessert case at the deli's rear wall.

"What are they?"

"*Pignoli* cookies."

"What's *pin-yoll?*" Mindy wrinkled her nose.

"Pine nuts."

"*Uck!* No way."

"Don't be rude, dear," said Celeste. "It's just that she's allergic to nuts."

"Well, technically, pine nuts are seeds," corrected Josie. She'd learned this handy factoid from Torre, who'd lately taken an interest in biology.

Mindy rattled off a well-rehearsed list. "I'm allergic to peanuts, walnuts, hazelnuts, almonds, pecans, Brazil nuts, *pine nuts,* and macadamia nuts."

"Ah, well. No *pignolis* for you, my friend," Josie said with grave sympathy.

Little Fawners, it seemed, were a gastronomically sensitive lot. Emily had already informed Josie that tonight she would have to provide an array of options for those who were gluten intolerant and lactose intolerant. In response she had laid in a supply of DeBoles artichoke pasta and planned to label every serving dish with care, lest some delicate soul end up writhing with stomach cramps or gasping for air in the emergency room. Now it seemed nuts were an issue as well. Josie wondered what was with all the intolerance. Where she came from, everyone was more than tolerant of all food, so long as it tasted good.

"How about some chocolate *cannoli*?" she asked. "Nut-free."

"Oh, no," said Celeste before Mindy could answer, "we'll take a half pound of the tuna and a quarter pound of the seafood salad. And by the way, there will be lots of green salad tonight at the party, won't there, Josie?"

"You bet." Emily had given her a heads up on this as well. Some carb-phobic mothers at the Spaghetti Night—and she knew she was looking at one of them—wouldn't touch the evening's eponymous dish if they were stranded on a desert island where spaghetti, and nothing else, grew on trees.

Josie rang up the Battins' lunches at the register and waved the mother-daughter duo off.

"See you tonight," Celeste chirped as she exited, managing to cast only one regretful backward glance at the chocolate cannoli.

Watching the blossoming Mindy in her skimpy shorts follow her mother out, Josie couldn't help but wonder for a moment just how interested in biology her own child had become. Then, with yet another topic to put out of her mind, she went back to stirring her sauce.

Outside, Celeste turned to Mindy. "Well, that was an interesting stopover, wasn't it? Hey, sweetie, how did you know about Billy Stand and the tuna salad?"

"Oh, you know, I sit next to Torre in English." She left out the part about sitting to the right of her left-handed classmate. It was a vantage point from which she could read his entire journal out of the corners of her lovely blue eyes.

• • •

Lydia was having some difficulty choosing among the three dresses she had laid out on her canopy bed. Was the tea length with the beaded border a bit too much for this "spaghetti" thing? Was it her imagination or did the coral mini-caftan make her look the tiniest bit teapot-ish? Finally, she settled on a salmon-hued strapless that fell just above the knee. Flinging a gaily-printed oversized silk scarf around the neckline, she deemed the accessory just the thing. Of course, the important matter tonight was not that she should look perfect—though she could hardly help it—but to ensure that Persephone's college application recommendations from the teachers would be nothing less than effusive.

She felt confident that one of them was in the bag. Madame Millefleur, Persey's French teacher, had responded to Lydia's initial feelers with a delighted "*Mais oui! Bien sûr!*" And why not? Persey had a true ear for the language, as evidenced by the fact that she could order fluently in Little Fawn's four-star waterfront bistro, *La Petite Biche*. But Persey also needed a math or science teacher to sing her praises.

Science was quite possibly out of the question. Biology had gone fairly well for her daughter until a lapse in attentiveness had led to the now infamous Country Day frog stampede. "*Mon Dieu! Toutes les grenouilles!*" Madame Millefleur had shrieked repeatedly over the public announcement system. And chemistry—well, that didn't bear consideration. Lydia was only grateful that no one had suffered worse than first-degree burns before Persey was banned from the lab altogether. So, math it was. Tonight she would have to settle things with Mr. Moskin once and for all.

"Hal," she called to her husband, who was still dawdling in the "His" bathroom of their master suite, "we really need to get going."

Hal tried sweeping a lock of his graying hair across his forehead, then put it back where it had been before, deciding he wasn't yet ready for a Trump-style comb-over. He examined his square jaw for any hint of stubble but found none. He straightened his Hugo Boss tie. He was a naturally handsome man who didn't usually take this long getting ready for an event, and certainly not for a Country Day fundraiser, but tonight Hal was determined to look flawlessly debonair. As he'd repeatedly told his old friend Preston Nobler, you had to look like money when you asked for money. And tonight, Nobler wouldn't be the only one asking.

"Coming, Lydia," he said.

As an afterthought, he plucked his transparent Invisalign braces from his mouth, as he had to do before every meal during his eighteen-month quest to procure an ever more winning smile. He exited the bathroom, and each spouse gave the other a thorough head-to-toe appraisal. They nodded simultaneously, each judging the other a suitable companion.

"Isn't Persephone coming?" Hal asked.

"She's already there. The caterer is that boy's mother—the one helping Persey with her SATs. She wanted to help them set up the buffet as a kind of thank you or something."

"Can't we just pay him?" Hal asked.

"That's what I said."

"Kids," said Hal. They just didn't understand the proper use of money.

• • •

Max Moskin sat in his small office at Little Fawn Country Day, working his way through a stack of math exams. He'd arrived at school hours before the Spaghetti Night festivities were due to begin. Truth be told, he probably would have spent much of

Saturday at school even if there had been no pending party to use as a rationalization, and no trigonometry tests to grade.

If Hannah, his ex-wife, were around, the two would have undoubtedly spent such a glorious autumn Saturday kayaking down the Navesink River, or maybe mountain biking at Hartshorne Woods. But Hannah wasn't coming back, and he just had to get used to it. Max's dedication to his teaching helped him cope with this sad reality.

He pulled the next math test from his pile and sighed. In its top right-hand corner, Persephone Thorn had drawn a smiley face next to her name. Maybe she thought it would bring her luck or cheer up her teacher. For a moment, it did sort of cheer him. Persey was a sweet, well-meaning girl who actually tried hard to grasp the concepts he taught, but she had no business being in his Advanced Trig/Pre-Calc class. Her placement level, like so many other things, had been insisted upon by her mother and in turn by Dr. Nobler.

He graded the test quickly, which was not difficult because Persey had neglected to answer the last five questions. Still, she'd grasped more than he'd hoped. He circled a grade of 76 next to her name and, in spite of himself, drew his own smiley emoticon beside hers. Tonight he'd have to face Mrs. Thorn and agree to write Persephone's college recommendation—Nobler had forewarned him. If only she weren't trying for Brown. God himself couldn't get into Brown these days.

The next test paper Max pulled from the stack belonged to Torre Messina. He shook his head in awe as he placed a check mark beside each answer and added ten points to Torre's grade of 100 for correctly tackling the multi-part extra credit question. Max had noticed that Torre had time to spare at the end of the exam, and had spent the last few minutes of the class period with his head on his desk catching a quick nap. If Max was still at Country Day next year, he'd have the boy in AP Calculus and, after that, in a Multivariable Calc tutorial. At least that was Dr. Nobler's plan.

But Max wasn't sure he'd be at Country Day much longer. This part of the world was no place for a newly single forty-four-year-old man. In the year since Hannah had left him, once the initial shock wore off, he'd begun sending resumes to high schools in New York City and Philadelphia. He was also taking the requisite courses that would qualify him as a school principal if such an opportunity arose. it would probably take him quite awhile to relocate with the economy the way it was. Still, that was the plan, and for all kinds of reasons—his personal funk being only one— he thought it was sound.

He prompted himself to stop dawdling and pulled another exam from his stack, but within a few moments an appetizing aroma distracted him. Out in the hallway he heard the clank and squeak of rolling wheels grow louder as the delicious scent grew stronger. Then, through the glass window in his office door, he saw none other than his students Persephone and Torre walk by. Looking at his watch, Max realized Spaghetti Night preparations must be underway. He had more work to do, but suddenly he couldn't resist following his nose. He opened the door and heard another clatter of rolling wheels round the corner. When a petite and rather attractive woman pushed a cart full of foil-covered trays into view, Max did the gentlemanly thing and offered a hand.

• • •

The headmaster was jubilant. Spaghetti Night was off to a ragingly good start. The school dining hall was transformed into a clubby setting by the pink lighting Celeste had suggested, and the food was a major success. Josie's marinara sauce was so rich it made even the "fake" artichoke pasta taste great, though he preferred the real fettuccini slathered in Bolognese, and that tangy linguini thing with the olives and lemon zest.

Despite the fact that the hospitality committee had opted not to serve alcohol this evening—there were children present, after all—everyone seemed in remarkably good spirits. Nobler hoped that would translate into open wallets. The ticket sales alone had netted his GOK campaign a tidy five-figure sum, but the take from the gift basket auction would significantly enhance it.

People were only too happy to overpay for donated goods when their friends and neighbors were watching.

Guests were already swarming around the ribbon-adorned baskets stuffed with goodies from local vendors. Little Fawn Linens, the Material Girl Salon, Peninsula Vintners, Diamond in the Rough Jewelers, and many more had given generously despite the lackluster economic climate. And why not? Nobler smiled to himself. Anyone could prosper by earning the loyalty of the Country Day crowd. Anyone.

Spearing the last of his tiny meatballs with a fork, Nobler excused himself from his table. "I'll be right back," he assured Hal Thorn and his other dining companions. "I just want to check and see how our little caterer is doing with the buffet." He wanted to make a special point of thanking Josie for her efforts, and perhaps he would snag second helpings of everything while he was at it, just to show his appreciation.

He began to make his way to the buffet station when he suddenly realized that this night was going to get even better. Billy and MaryAnn Stand had actually shown up—at his fundraiser! Clutching his empty plate tighter, Nobler used his free hand to mop his brow with his napkin. He scurried over to the famous couple who stood canoodling with Josie over a hot tray of gnocchi. *So,* he thought, *the rumors they're old friends must be true.*

"Why, Mr. and Mrs. Stand," he enthused. "Why, how good of you to join us. Why, aren't you kind to come? Why, why..."

Incredibly, he found himself at a loss for words. He'd met briefly with the Stands when the couple had registered their twins for kindergarten and done what he felt was an admirable job of maintaining professionalism. All the while a part of him had wanted nothing more than to sway, shout, and clap his hands with the same fervor he'd felt the first time he saw Billy perform at Madison Square Garden so many years before. Of course, the milligram of Xanax he'd popped before their meeting hadn't hurt his ability to restrain himself.

But tonight his cup ranneth over, and he'd taken no sedative to stop its flow. Imagine if the Stands were actually going to be involved parents, school supporters, and even Givers of

Knowledge—well, the sky was his limit. He could build this school to no end and that damned Lady of Perpetual Sorrows could cry herself a river. Yeah, maybe *she* should pop a Xanax.

"Hey, no problem." Billy snapped him out of his reverie. "We all gotta eat."

"Well, indeed we do. Indeed," he agreed. "And isn't this food just scrumptious? Superb!" *Aarrgghh.* He was babbling again. He fought the urge to bite down on his tongue.

"*Mmm,*" said Billy, and Josie could have sworn he shot her the tiniest wink. "Sauce like her mama used to make."

"Well, that explains it," Nobler offered. "Tradition! Nothing like it! Nothing!"

"Yup," agreed Billy.

"Word!" Nobler chimed. Ah, that was better. He'd come up with a cool phrase a dude like Billy would appreciate. Good thing he routinely spied on his students' Facebook pages; it helped him keep up with the lingo.

"Say," he ventured, emboldened, "why don't you two join me at my table? I'd love to introduce you to our hospitality committee."

Billy glanced at his wife, who in turn glanced at Josie. "Aren't you going to eat, Josie?" MaryAnn asked. "Come sit with us, okay? I don't know a soul here except you."

"Me?" said Josie, surprised by the invitation. Until tonight, she and MaryAnn hadn't crossed paths in twenty years. Even back in Wild Bay, they'd only known one another casually. By the time Billy was dating the shy, pretty girl from the parochial high school on the "better" side of town, Josie was wrapped up in her romance with Sal. It was funny how it had all turned out.

"I don't think I can leave my post." She gestured to the crowded buffet table. "Excuse me a sec," she added, turning her attention to her young helpers. "Hey, Torre honey, can you and Persey please refill the salad platter?"

Just then she felt a hand on her shoulder. She turned and looked up into the kind eyes of Max Moskin.

"Mrs. Messina here has done enough, don't you all agree?" Max mustered up the avuncular yet authoritative teacher tone he'd perfected over the course of his career. "Take a break, Josie. I'll hold down the fort."

"Oh, no, Mr. Moskin, you've done too much already," she replied. He had pitched in with a vengeance from the moment she'd encountered him in the hallway, wheeling carts of trays up from the van, laying out tablecloths and silverware, and keeping the Sterno flames lit.

"Nonsense. It's my pleasure," he insisted. He'd had more fun pitching in with Josie and the kids than he'd had in quite a while. Besides, operating the buffet table meant he might be able to dodge Persephone's mom awhile longer.

"Let me start by fixing you a plate, Josie."

"Oh, okay. Well, just a little," she relented. "I've been picking all day." Everyone wondered how she stayed so slim when she spent so many hours in the kitchen. The truth was that by the time she finished preparing a dish, tasting it along the way, she had little appetite for it. It was as if she had inoculated herself against temptation. Her satisfaction came from watching others enjoy what she had prepared.

Nobler was already steering the Stands toward the table he shared with the Thorns, the Luffhausers, and Celeste Battin. The place reserved for Andy Battin sat empty; he had been delayed once again in "Honk Kong or Mekong or King Kong," as Celeste had explained it. In a hospitable frenzy, more chairs were quickly rounded up to accommodate Billy, MaryAnn, and the increasingly popular Mrs. Messina.

When Josie arrived with her plate, which Max had filled with more than she could possibly eat, she was beckoned by the headmaster toward the one remaining empty spot between him and Hal. Hal extended his hand, smiled dazzlingly and somewhat convincingly, and boomed his name in her ear.

Across the table, Billy looked like the meat in a Luffhauser sandwich, so closely were Emily and Brad leaning in toward him. Josie had a hunch she knew the Luffhausers' agenda. Emily had already confided in Josie about her brilliant plan to get Billy to perform at a benefit for the Wild Bay Food Bank. It was an obvious match, and Billy was well known for his charitable generosity.

In the years when he'd forsaken the Jersey shore for Hollywood, an entire wing of a Los Angeles children's hospital was named for him. Now he was back, and Emily would be damned if she didn't whet this homeboy's philanthropic appetite for some worthy local causes.

Josie toyed with a forkful of linguine, hoping that Max was making sure the sauce tureens were full. To her left, she could hear the headmaster giving his undivided attention, between bites, to MaryAnn.

"Fantastic opportunity...enjoying all the new facilities for years to come... those adorable twins of yours...perhaps their future baby brothers or sisters...pre-pre-kindergarten...an incomparable jumpstart."

MaryAnn's eyes looked a bit glazed. She was nodding politely, almost like a Bobblehead doll, Josie thought. Well, she supposed Dr. Nobler could induce that kind of reaction in almost anyone.

Beside her, Hal cleared his throat; apparently he'd come up with something to say to Josie other than his own name. "The food's great," he said, mindful that flattery was always a good conversational gambit. Actually, he was mildly worried that the tomato sauce might stain his bicuspids, which he'd just had laser whitened.

"Thanks," said Josie.

He leaned in a little closer. "Say, I understand you know our local rock star."

"Oh, very little," she said. Gosh, things got around. "I knew his family a long, long time ago."

"Well, so that's *her*, isn't it? The one from the song?" he asked, glancing toward MaryAnn.

The question was rhetorical, Josie knew. Any red-blooded American who hadn't been living in a cave for the past two decades—and maybe even a few who had—knew that MaryAnn Stand, née MaryAnn Noone, was the inspiration for Billy's first hit song, "Slow Down, MaryAnn." The couple's teenage romance and its adult resurrection many years later had made the cover of not only *People*, but also *Rolling Stone* and *Time*. None of this prevented Hal from proving to Josie that he, too, was in the know.

Miming a discreet bit of air guitar, he sang a bit too loudly in Josie's ear.

> *"Slow down, slow down, MaryAnn*
> *In your plaid of greens and blues*
> *I think I see the Holy Grail*
> *reflected in your patent leather shoes"*

"Yup, that's the one," Josie agreed, wondering how she could keep him from moving on to the second verse. "Are you a musician, Hal?"

"Me? Ha! Well, er, no. Obviously not," he said, taking the bait. "I'm in chairs."

"You're in *chairs?*"

He reached for a business card and handed it to Josie. *Harold Thorn, CEO, Ergo-Geri Inc.*

"Ergonomically correct loungers for seniors. Got everything the shrivs could ever want built right in: reading lights, headphone jacks, seat heaters, flip-out trays, and battery-operated personal massagers for rehabilitative physical therapy. Off the record, I call them my Stephen Hawking specials. Ha! Put Grandma in one of these things and she'll gladly stay in it all day. I tell you we're minting money down in Florida. Just coining it."

"Shrivs?"

"Yeah, you know, geezers. The shriveled ones."

"Oh...I see." She shuddered slightly as she mentally fast-forwarded forty years into the future, picturing Torre plopping her into a nursing home lounge chair as he and her adorable grandkids waved good-bye.

"You know, it's funny you should want to know about this," Hal went on, "because you see we're actually raising private equity at the moment to—"

"Oh? Isn't that wonderful? Well, I've really got to go and check on—" Josie craned her neck to see how Max was getting along. "I think...maybe it's time to put out the desserts."

But just then, the headmaster stood and excused himself from the table once more. Mrs. Chapel began flicking the overhead lights, signaling the onset of another fundraising pitch. Lydia, the former psych major, noted that the flickering was rapidly becoming a neo-Pavlovian signal that induced in parents a strong urge to cleave tightly to their wallets.

Good thing he was pumped and carbo-loaded, Nobler thought. Tonight he was planning to introduce his latest brainstorm: A full IMAX theatre for the school's new multimedia center—with 3-D capabilities! All the better for watching those award-winning science documentaries. Why make everyone schlep into the Museum of Natural History on those god-awful field trips when his students could watch Galapagos tortoises and…whatever…without ever leaving their insular peninsula?

Josie was wondering if it would be rude to lay out the dessert spread while the headmaster gave what she knew would be a long-winded speech. Just then, though, she saw MaryAnn get up and head toward the exit to the ladies' lounge. Not a bad idea. Josie decided to duck in herself and miss a bit of the—what had Emily called it?—bloviating.

In the ladies' room, she found MaryAnn perched on the edge of a counter of sinks that ran along the wall. She stopped fishing for something in her purse when Josie entered.

"Hey, Josie," she said in what still sounded like the soft voice of the shy teenage girl she'd been. "We barely got to say hello before. It's been a while."

"I'll say, but you'd never know it to look at you."

It was almost true. Put MaryAnn back in her Saint Teresa's school uniform and you'd be tempted to hand her milk money and a pencil box—unless, of course, you happened to notice the dark circles and puffiness under her eyes. Josie chalked these up as telltale signs of motherhood—and of twins, no less.

MaryAnn deflected the compliment. "Hey, you're the one who's looking great, and that son of yours is adorable."

"I'm biased," said Josie. "Hey, did you know I met the twins? Billy brought them into my deli."

"Really? He did?" MaryAnn seemed surprised to hear it.

"They're the image of you."

"Only on the outside," she said. "Personality-wise they're all Billy. Maybe school will soak up of some of their excess energy."

"Well, kids, you know. I wouldn't count on it."

"Has your son been at this school a long time?"

"Oh no, just started this year. We're newbies, like you."

"Wow, small world," said MaryAnn distractedly. She began to rummage through her purse again.

"Well, excuse me a sec," said Josie. She glanced at her watch and made for a bathroom stall. At some point Dr. Nobler would wind down, and the guests would start trolling for a sugar high to counter his soporific effect.

When Josie emerged, MaryAnn was gone. Back in the dining hall, the headmaster was wrapping up his remarks with an unexpected surprise.

"And now, as a special delight—before we get to what I'm told are some outstanding sweets—I've just been informed that seventh grader Mindy Battin is going to grace us with a song. So here, um, without further ado, is Miss Battin singing..." He looked toward Celeste, who mouthed something in his direction. "Oh, yes...and, my goodness, what an appropriate choice it is. Here's our Mindy with 'For a Moment Like This.'"

Nobler was determined to seem unsurprised by the impromptu program addition. Such spontaneity, he assured himself, was the inevitable result of his creativity-promoting curriculum. *That's how we roll here at Country Day.*

Celeste fumbled momentarily with the buttons on a large boom box as Mindy, dressed in a Juicy Couture bright fuchsia ruffled tank dress over black leggings, stood serenely in the center of the room, looking like a page out of *Teen Vogue*. If the girl possessed a scintilla of performance anxiety, she did a magnificent job of concealing it. When a karaoke-style instrumental backup began, she flipped her hair and emphatically burst into song.

"For a momennnt like thissssss..."

Almost all eyes were on the thirteen-year-old diva—but not everyone's. Lydia affixed her gaze on Max. It was clever of him to hide in plain sight the way he had this evening, but she was cleverer by half. There was still time to secure his promise of a glowing recommendation for Persey tonight; she would do so, regardless of how many party guests, foodstuffs, and auction items stood in her way.

"Some people wait a liiiiifetimme…"

Hal eyed Brad, admiring the cut of the man's suit, especially its deep, deep Luffhauser pockets. No matter what the state of the economy, Hal was sure that banker Brad had a nice chunk of change lying around to invest in Ergo-Geri's initial public offering. There was no time like the present to make his case; in fact, he might have very little time left at all before…

"Some people search foreeeeverrrr…"

Celeste proudly beamed most of her attention to her talented offspring, except for the teeny sliver of consciousness she reserved for tracking Marisa Markle's whereabouts. Tonight the temptress had mingled shamelessly amidst the crowd. Celeste had turned her back, and surreptitiously popped a tortellini between her teeth, when Markle had had the audacity to stop by her table for a moment to gush at Billy Stand that his twins were "positively blooming" in her kindergarten class.

"For a mommmmennnnt…"

Billy's eyes searched the crowd for his wife, who was—*oh God, not again*—missing in action. He made a small apologetic wave in Emily's direction before heading toward the door. He hoped he could track MaryAnn down before anyone else did.

"A mommmmeeeeeent like thiiiisss."

Mindy's performance—or at any rate the conclusion of it—elicited fervent applause. And with desserts and gift baskets in the offing, the Spaghetti Night revelers went off in search of their quarries.

• • •

Language Arts Journal, October 18
Mindy Battin

Stupid party. Stupid stupid song. <u>I felt ridiculous</u>. What's the point when the one person I wanted to hear me wasn't even there?

Never mind. I will get his attention. No matter what. <u>I feel one hundred percent sure.</u>

Make that one hundred and ten.

<u>I'm feeling like I've got a plan</u>.

Persephone Thorn

Supplement to the Common Application

Why Brown?

I have always known I would go to Brown. My mother dressed me in teeny Brown T-shirts from Ivy Sport when I was just a toddler. I have a picture of me dressed like that hanging over my desk, so I can never forget that I am supposed to go to your school. Not for a minute, not even when I try. The truth is, I don't really look all that great in brown, if you really want to know. And anyone who says it's the new black is just kidding herself…

Why Brown?

I would like to attend Brown because I hear you have an open curriculum and I can take all your courses pass/fail. Then my parents could never nag me about my grades. For all they would know I could be acing rocket science. LOL

Why Brown?

I love bears. You know, like your big brown mascot. I mean, here at Little Fawn our mascot is—guess what?—a baby deer. Duh. I mean, that's a little on the nose if you ask me. I'm so over the Bambi thing. But you guys…

Why Brown?

Why? Why? Why???????

CHAPTER 4:

Parent - Teacher Conferences

October 24
FROM: Dr. Preston Nobler
TO: All Faculty
RE: Parent-Teacher Conferences

As I gaze from my office window at a most colorful convocation of autumn leaves languidly drifting toward earth, where they shall snap, crackle, and pop beneath our students' scampering feet, I am reminded that, once again, fall parent-teacher conferences are upon us. As Madame Millefleur says: *Bon courage*!

Please remember, we view parental interfaces as opportunities to:

1) *Manage Expectations*: While not every child exceeds expectations in every subject (and some, I daresay, in none), we here at LFCD are determined to unearth every student's special gift, no matter how obscure or miniscule. Please remind over-anxious parents, particularly those fixated on so-called "objective measures" such as standardized test scores or college admissions,

that our mission is not to produce academic automatons, but rather to stimulate the innate drive for lifelong learning (LLL).

2) *Encourage Goal-Setting*: Parents should be urged to set goals with their children and to serve as role models for follow-through. To this end, what could be better than parents committing to be selfless and generous Givers of Knowledge? (Please note that Capital Campaign brochures will be discretely placed in the Steuben bowls in the various waiting areas.)

3) *Solicit Feedback*: We are always interested in what parents have to say. Please note especially any comments—direct or indirect—regarding the potential transfer of students to Our Lady of Perpetual Sorrows. I wish to know immediately of any negative comparison, no matter how offhand, of our academic standing as compared to that of OLPS.

With further regard to feedback, let me here address a somewhat delicate matter. As some of you might be aware, a small incident of pilferage transpired at our recent Spaghetti Night auction. The winners of the bidding on a basket donated by Peninsula Vintners were dismayed to find that the basket had been tampered with, and one of its contents—a bottle of twenty-five-year-old Sauterne that the merchant noted would "reveal alternating notes of vanilla, spicy cherry, and smoky butterscotch"—had been removed. Reparations to the generous bidders have of course been made, and we feel certain the matter was simply the result of a student prank; nevertheless, we hope to identify the perpetrator(s). Should your upcoming discussions happen to reveal any information, or hint thereof, kindly alert me—in confidence—ASAP!

Billy stared into his near-empty refrigerator. He couldn't possibly make a meal for the twins out of ketchup, lettuce, orange juice, and string cheese, could he? He glanced at the wall clock: 6 p.m. He'd have to leave for Country Day in less than an hour to make parent-teacher conference night on time. That left him with a number of knotty problems to solve in less than sixty minutes.

MaryAnn had taken to bed, saying she felt a head cold coming on, and announced that she wasn't up to going anywhere tonight. To top it off, another housekeeper had quit the day before and the cupboards were bare. The kids had no sitter and no supper.

In the back of his mind, Billy began to hear a tune. *Thump thumpa tha dum. Thump thumpa tha dum.* It was often this way; the music would come when he was feeling low, when he needed to sort something out. Some said it was his blessing; sometimes it felt like his curse. Whatever it was and wherever it came from, here it was.

He began to hum under his breath, his left foot tapping out a beat. Billy was left-footed the way others were left-handed. Somehow his foot always got involved in the creation of his songs. The lyrics were coming too, about a "star" who turned out to be a loser at love and marriage in a world that thought his holding onto a woman would be easy. *What a joke.* Of course the song, if it ever came together, wouldn't tell the literal story. He'd made that mistake once long ago—and the results still haunted him—but he was older and wiser now. He'd play with the sad truth, shape it, pare it, obfuscate it and, of course, punctuate it with a really catchy chorus.

Who would have believed the real story anyway? None of his self-appointed biographers had gotten it quite right—not even that douchebag in L.A. who had systematically rummaged through his trash cans for so many years. Everyone knew that Billy Stand had become a national phenomenon when he was only eighteen, catapulting from the Jersey shore club scene to national acclaim. Many of his fans could even recite, with varying degrees of accuracy, the story of his debut at the Sea Wall in Belmar.

Billy wasn't even supposed to take the stage that night—or any night as far as the club owner, Phil Yobst, was concerned. Jaded by the throaty warbles of too many Springsteen wannabes, "Philly Yo," as everyone called him, was determined to break out of a musical rut. No more pretty boy guitar strummers for him. It was the cusp of the 1990s, and the Billboard charts were thick with lithe and lyrical girls. Surely somewhere in Jersey the next Mariah, Madonna, or Paula was ripe for picking, and he was determined to discover her.

After a long, thorough search, Philly thought he had found the one. Sadly, it turned out the promising young woman, who called herself Epiphany, was in the end more interested in procuring Quaaludes than in pursuing a singing career. On her much promoted big night, somewhere between the Sea Wall's parking lot and the club's back door, she walked into the side of a dumpster, chipped two front teeth, and collapsed in a heap behind a Subaru Legacy. Two hours later, Epiphany regained consciousness in Philly Yo's office and, true to her stage moniker, had a consciousness-altering insight. The life of a rock star was not for her. She would do as her parents had pleaded: go to Brookdale Community College and study to become a radiology technician.

It was just as well, for by that time Philly had spotted Billy Stand, one of those perennial guitar-slinging pests, in the crowd. Having no other option, he asked the young hopeful to step in. Billy played the songs he'd worked out in his head all those times he'd been hollered at for not paying attention in high school. Within fifteen minutes, he had won the heart of every girl and the grudging respect of every guy in the packed house. The air in the club sizzled, just like in the moments before a northeaster slammed into the shore. Little Billy Stankiewicz, placed behind a microphone, evinced a profound gravitational pull over everyone in his orbit. Suddenly, everyone at the Sea Wall just knew: this was no wannabe; this was an original.

It all happened so fast. Philly knew every talented musician south of Raritan Bay. He introduced Billy—whose name quickly morphed from Stankiewicz to its abbreviated version—to bass player Danny Krakowski and drummer Tony Bonodaro. In what was later regarded in the music industry as a true stroke of genius musical matchmaking, he also matched him up with saxophonist Moses Jones, the hulking former Rutgers football star who, to the deep consternation of the New York Giants, had chosen the uncertainty of a life in rock and roll over a multi-million dollar NFL contract. Soon Billy Stand and the newly christened C-Side Band had three singles on the charts, the most popular of which was the plaintive "Slow Down MaryAnn."

Now came the parts of the story that remained and would remain private—at least Billy hoped. When the band embarked on the first of their cross-country tours, he beseeched MaryAnn to go along. But she was not yet eighteen and her parents hit the ceiling, insisting that their straight-A student enroll at Villanova as they'd long planned.

Billy swore eternal allegiance, but not even a heart as true as his and devotion as strong as MaryAnn's could weather the interminable separations and the ever-widening gap between the lovers' day-to-day realities. MaryAnn got a B.A. in Education and an M.A. in Counseling Psychology. Billy got married.

He had never been much for the groupie scene. For better or worse, that turf was more than thoroughly mined by Tony, Danny, and Moses—until Moses had a vision on the Santa Monica Freeway, totaled his Porsche, and fervently embraced the Lord. When Billy met Annabelle Mercer, star of the smash sitcom *Say Aaaah*, at a Hollywood Hills after-concert party, he was instantly as smitten as the millions of male fans who routinely tuned in to her weekly series. (Their reasons had little to do with its plot line, such as it was, about the trials and tribulations of three hapless but endearing female medical students.)

Even so many years later, tapping out a tune in his Little Fawn kitchen, Billy felt a wave of bittersweet nostalgia wash over him as he recalled the early stages of his union with Annabelle. The two had bought a sprawling house in Malibu Colony, and Billy added two film-scoring Oscars to his growing cache of Grammys. But their happy union hadn't lasted long.

When Annabelle was offered a dramatic role in a movie with clear Oscar potential, she'd bailed on her sitcom and, with Billy's enthusiastic support, had headed off to shoot on location in Tasmania. By the time Billy arrived to visit his wife on the set nearly three months later, she had reached two irrevocable conclusions: First, she was indeed a serious and gifted actress; and second, she had fallen in love with her co-star, who also happened to be a very serious and gifted actress.

Billy tapped his foot in time with a lyric that popped into his head:

Some losers lose to other guys
Some losers lose to luck
Some lose their girls to other girls
Who I guess are a better—

He laughed aloud, cheering up for a moment. Nah. He sure wasn't gonna write *that*. But he was at least entitled to amuse himself, wasn't he? God knows he had few lighthearted moments lately, with his second marriage seemingly on the brink.

What was it with MaryAnn? Why was she ruining it all? Neither one of them could believe their luck when they managed to find one another again. Billy had been playing a concert in Philadelphia and MaryAnn had come. She hadn't told him; she hadn't even planned to see him. It had simply been too long, and she had relegated their relationship to the category of "once upon a time." She wouldn't have gone to the concert at all, but escorting the glee club of Wild Bay High School, where she worked a guidance counselor, fell to her when both the chorale director and the assistant principal succumbed to chicken pox.

When Billy's publicist found out a group of kids from Wild Bay had bussed in, she thought it would make a nice photo op. And the rest—at least the good part—rapidly became the stuff of pop legend: The lovers, torn asunder, reunited. The hometown sweethearts fulfilling their destiny as soul mates. The woman who inspired the song that started it all joining with the man whose slow burn of love had never quite extinguished. No one could resist Billy and MaryAnn's fairy tale. *Maybe not even the two of us*, thought Billy.

Billy stopped his humming and tapping and shook his head as if to jar the unwelcome idea from his brain. Deep down he believed, or at least hoped, his life with MaryAnn was meant to be. And little Lucy and Harry were the lights of his world. He'd thought that moving back from L.A. to their home turf would help—MaryAnn never counted the Malibu shore as the "real" shore—but so far it hadn't. Now he just didn't know what to do about the darkness that seemed to be enveloping his wife. Hell, he didn't even know what to do about dinner, or about finding a sitter on short notice.

He pulled his cell phone from his pocket and scanned his list of contacts. It read like a Who's Who of rock royalty, movie stars, left-leaning politicians whose campaigns he'd stomped for, and music business movers and shakers. Most of the numbers had California, New York, or D.C. area codes, but none would do him any good tonight. He knew no one nearby who could help him out of a last-minute workaday jam.

Then again, maybe he did. He pressed 411 and asked for the number of Cooler at the Shore.

• • •

Josie and Billy were late arriving at Little Fawn Country Day, and Mrs. Chapel, charged by the headmaster with keeping things moving in an orderly fashion, clucked reprovingly. "My, but you two are soaking wet," she pointed out, somewhat unnecessarily.

"Yup, it's cats and dogs out there, ma'am," Billy said. "Just started when we were parking."

Josie pulled a small pack of tissues from her handbag, tore off its plastic sheath, and handed half the contents to Billy. He grinned at the maternal gesture and began dabbing his face.

Mrs. Chapel repressed a sigh. It wasn't going to help the general mood of the evening if all the latecomers—and there were always a number of them—were waterlogged. It certainly wouldn't predispose parents to pass their waiting time *ooh*-ing and *ahh*-ing over the elegant new Givers of Knowledge brochures. All students were required to fulfill yearly school service hours, which they unilaterally referred to as slave labor; she'd have to find one of them to rustle up some towels from the gymnasium. Meanwhile, she'd do her best to strictly enforce the ten-minute conference limit starting right now.

"Mr. Stand, can I ask you to go right through that door and straight down the hall to the Lower School area? Miss Markle will be with you shortly," she said briskly. It sounded less like a request than a marching order, and Billy, who had always been intimidated by schools and the petty tyrants who ran them, reflexively obeyed.

"Mrs. Messina," she said, handing Josie a printed schedule, "I see you've requested to speak with Mr. Moskin and Mr. Jakes. Mr. Moskin will see you first. In fact"—she glanced at the wall clock and furrowed her eyebrows—"he should be ready for you right now. Follow me and we'll see what's keeping him."

Josie, still dripping, followed her resolute leader, who moved at a power walk clip toward Max's math classroom. Mrs. Chapel eyeballed the sign-in sheet on the door and frowned as she noted Lydia's Thorn's bold backhand signature. "We'll give them just one more minute," she told Josie. "Wait here. I'll be back."

Inside Room 216, Max sat silently as Lydia read the letter of recommendation he had finally penned for her daughter. He had every right to keep such letters private, since Persephone, as per standard practice, had waived her right to view his evaluation. Had it been a year ago, Max might well have summoned up the nerve to tell Lydia this was really none of her business. But tonight he'd waved the white flag. The fight had gone out of him, though he nursed the strong hope that by this time next year he'd be at another school, maybe one that placed its highest value on education—if such a place existed anymore.

Lydia pulled a pen from her purse. "You don't mind a few suggestions, do you?"

"Suggest away." *In for a penny, in for a pound,* thought Max. While Lydia scribbled, he eyed his evening schedule. Josie Messina was next; maybe she was already waiting for him. The thought cheered him. It was always a pleasure to talk with the parent of such a talented student. Besides, upbeat and down-to-earth Josie would be the perfect counterpoint to stick-up-her-butt Lydia. Max looked at his watch and realized just how eager he was to end his current session.

"Lydia, why don't you take your time with that and leave it in my mailbox?" he suggested.

"Oh, I'm just finishing." Lydia handed him her notes. "Nothing major. I'm just wondering if you could say Persephone was 'the most improved' in your class rather than 'much improved.' Has a better ring, don't you think?"

Max considered a moment. "Done," he agreed. After all, Persey had been trying hard lately, and Torre was tutoring her in classwork now that the SATs were over. In truth, the girl had come along the furthest of anyone in class—if only because she'd had the furthest distance to cover.

"Wonderful," said Lydia. She graciously offered Max her hand in parting, and her gesture coincided with Mrs. Chapel's impatient rap on the door.

Lydia and Josie edged past each other in the doorway as they swapped places. "Sorry," Josie mouthed, rolling her eyes in Mrs. Chapel's direction.

"Goodness," said Lydia aloud. "What happened to you, Josie dear? You look like a drowned kitten."

"Just a little rain," Mrs. Chapel answered on Josie's behalf. "Let's keep moving, ladies. *Tempus fugit.* Time's a wastin'. "

Mrs. Chapel closed the door behind Josie with a resounding click, and Josie couldn't help but giggle.

"What's with that woman and the Latin?"

Max chuckled. He'd long wondered the same thing. "Dead language Tourettes?" he offered.

Josie rewarded him with a hearty laugh.

"I was going to get her a T-shirt. '*Omnia dicta fortiori, si dicta Latin.*' It means 'Everything sounds better in Latin.'"

"Do it!" said Josie.

Max beamed. Hey, maybe he *would* do it. What the heck?

About to offer Josie a chair, he realized she was still dripping and shivering from her run through the storm. "Mrs. Messina…"

"Josie, remember?"

"Josie, you can't stay in those clothes all evening. Say, why don't you give me just a minute—I have an idea." He opened the classroom door. "Back in a flash."

Practically loping down the hall, Max retrieved from his office a navy blue hooded fleece zip-up with LFCD's crest emblazoned on it. He often wore it when he came in to work on weekends and the building's heat thermostat was set low. He raced back and offered it.

"Why don't you take off your blouse and put this on, Josie? I mean, er—" He blushed beet red, which Josie found adorable. "I'll step out for another minute. Open the door when you're, you know, decent."

Josie smiled. She'd been in full-out mom mode for so many years, and she couldn't remember the last time anyone had looked after her this way. She did as Max asked, after which the two had a convivial and, in the opinion of the lurking Mrs. Chapel, far too lengthy conversation about Torre's mathematical abilities (excellent), his adjustment to LFCD (very good), and his willingness to help other students who were not as facile with math as he was (outstanding). Their conversation was so pleasant that Max surprised even himself by suggesting they continue it at the evening's end over coffee, or maybe even a nightcap.

Josie was sincere when she said she'd like to do it another time. "I gave someone a lift here and I've got to drive him home and pick up Torre. Torre's babysitting at his house."

"Of course," Max said. "I understand. Maybe I could, um, you know, give you a call?"

"Sure," she agreed, only the tiniest bit flustered. "I mean, that would be nice? Okay then, well, um, you know, I better go? *Tempus fugit,* or whatever."

"Whatever!" he echoed cheerfully.

Josie might have wished for a moment to take in what had just happened—it had been years since anyone asked her out on a date, if that's what Max had actually just done—but for now, the luxury of reverie eluded her. A student volunteer, one of the Luffhauser boys, noticed her perplexity and, thinking she was lost, politely insisted on looking at her schedule and steering her in the direction of the computer science classroom, where Benjamin Jakes greeted her.

A bald, pale beanpole of a man with uncommonly thick eyeglasses, Benjamin Jakes looked every inch the computer geek. Josie knew how much her son loved computers, but she fervently hoped his predilection would never result in a complexion as pasty as Jakes's. The man looked like he hadn't spent an hour in the sunshine since first grade recess.

Jakes seemed a little fidgety, which Josie chalked up to her running behind their appointed time. The instructor cracked the knuckles of his cigarette-stained fingers as he ushered her to a student chair at one of the computer stations. He drew another chair across from her—*a little too close*, she thought—turned it around, and straddled it with his gangly legs.

"So," he said, fixing her with a stare from behind his weighty lenses, "you are the wonder boy's mommy dearest. How does it feel?"

"Uh, good, I guess?"

"I'll bet it does feel good." He nodded. "Some people can devote their whole life to a single pursuit and not come close to Torre's natural abilities. *Their entire life.*"

Josie registered the edge in Jakes's voice; it wasn't a tone totally unfamiliar to her. While many adults were impressed with her son's aptitude, she had run into a few who actually seemed to resent him. Not everyone loved a prodigy, it turned out—especially not those who, for whatever reason, might be a little insecure about the path their own life had taken. But she knew Torre loved this class and valued Mr. Jakes's opinion. For her son's sake, she resorted to stroking the teacher's ego.

"Well, it's certainly gratifying to hear that coming from someone with your expertise."

Jakes fixed her with an even harder stare. *What could this woman know about his expertise?* Surely that blowhard Nobler hadn't told anyone about his background. No, he couldn't have. That would jeopardize his own agenda, and even Nobler wasn't that stupid. Besides, the U.S. Attorney's office hadn't been able to make the corporate espionage charge stick. Technically, he was clean as a whistle.

"So, uh, I hope Torre is doing well in your seminar?" Josie realized she'd better pick up the ball when he didn't reply to her gambit.

At this, Jakes began to chuckle. Actually, Josie thought it was more of a giggle. "*Well?*" he repeated. "Yes, he's doing well. But then again, you knew he would."

"Gee, I wasn't really sure how he'd do. The adjustment and all? And it's a really advanced class, isn't it? You know, I'm really just hoping he can help me get my store's accounts on Quicken one of these days."

"Quicken? Mrs. Messina," Jakes practically snorted, "surely anyone who could hack into his middle school's network and alter students' report card printouts can handle that, right?"

Josie was flabbergasted. Dr. Nobler had promised her that Torre's Incident at Lower Fawn Middle School would never be divulged at Country Day. What did the headmaster tell Jakes, and had he told anyone else? She thought he'd understood that they wanted to close that unfortunate chapter. Besides, Dr. Nobler had agreed that Torre's motives were pure, even if his methods were somewhat questionable.

"Mr. Jakes, I—well—" Josie stammered. "You know that was just a prank. Regrettable, of course, and Torre owned up to it completely. It's just—well, there were a few boys that were always bullying him and his friends."

Jakes nodded and rubbed his palms together as if relishing the details of Torre's transgression. "Oh, yes, I know. After Torre's little intervention, the bullies all got straight F's and unsatisfactories in conduct. Served them right, the little thugs. The teacher wouldn't have had the *coyones* to do it."

Josie supposed she ought to have felt relieved. His tension seemed to have evaporated. Contrary to judging her son harshly, he seemed almost gleeful at the thought of Torre's hacking hijinks. Maybe this was just the way computer nerds got their jollies, but something about the teacher's attitude made her ill at ease and she attempted to change the subject.

"So, what are you guys working on in here? It certainly looks high tech." She waved her hand to indicate fifteen state of the art workstations, each equipped with both a PC and a Mac.

"Oh, open infrastructure, core applications, remote procedure calls—you know." Jakes's now perfunctory tone indicated that he was quite sure she didn't understand a word of what he was saying, and she sensed that was the way he liked it.

"Super," she said. "And Torre says you're working in teams?"

"Yes, we are. Revolving teams. Keeps it fresh, you know. Good for brainstorming. And Torre is about to be my teammate on a new project."

"Really!" Josie exclaimed. She guessed that was a good thing, and didn't quite know why this bit of news gave her a creepy feeling. "You're sure he's up to that?"

There was Jakes's little giggle again. "Really, Mrs. Messina. Well, you are just a delight, aren't you?" He regarded her for a long moment from behind his convex eyeglasses before pronouncing their parent-teacher session at an end. "I'm afraid I have to move along now, or Mrs. Chapel will have my head," he apologized.

"Oh, I completely understand," Josie said. Her talks with both Max and Jakes had gone significantly beyond their appointed ten minutes, and it suddenly occurred to her that Billy, who had only one teacher on his schedule, might already be waiting for her.

Just as she reached for the computer lab doorknob, Jakes stopped her with an afterthought. "Oh, by the way, Mrs. Messina, wonderful job on Spaghetti Night. Speaking of which, you wouldn't happen to know anything about a certain bottle of wine that happened to vanish from one of the gift baskets, would you?"

"Excuse me?"

"Oh, it was just some harmless prank, I'm sure," he said. "I just thought I'd ask since you were in the thick of things that night—you and your little helpers."

"Well, I don't have a clue about anything like that," she said. She was feeling more uncomfortable than before, and she hadn't thought that was possible. "But as you say, it sounds like a harmless prank, doesn't it?"

"Of course." He smiled. "Never mind anyhow. Kids. Forget I mentioned it."

Josie made her way out to the marble-floored main lobby where she and Billy had agreed to meet, but Billy was nowhere in sight. That was all right with her; she had plenty to think about. She mulled over Max's overture. She worried whether anyone other than Jakes and Dr. Nobler knew about Torre's sixth grade indiscretion. She brooded that Torre might become the scapegoat for every unsolved student crime at Country Day. She was so preoccupied that she barely noticed it was nearly another half an hour before Billy, looking warm, dry, and happy, emerged from Miss Markle's gaily decorated kindergarten classroom.

• • •

Language Arts Journal, October 25 Torre Messina

Last night I babysat for Lucy and Harry Stand. It was really fun, even though <u>I felt kind of weird about doing it since I never babysat before</u>. But Mom said we had to help the Stands out of a jam and Billy said he figured I had the "babysitting gene" like my mother.

I actually had a great time. The three of us ate the dinner my mom brought over and then I played with them. Those kids are really funny, and they are really good at Wii Sports – for kindergartners. They've also got every single Thomas the Tank Engine train and about a mile of track. They've got the whole third floor of their house set up as a huge playroom. It was so cool <u>I almost felt jealous of them</u>. But they are really so nice that I got over it. For a while I pretended they were my little brother and sister. I always wanted brothers and sisters. <u>Sometimes I feel lonely</u>.

After a while, Mrs. Stand came upstairs and hung out with us. She was really nice too. I was surprised to see her because my mom said she was sick and would be in bed and that I should only get her in an emergency. But Mrs. Stand didn't seem sick at all. At least not after she found that bottle of butterscotchy-smelling cough medicine she was looking for in the bottom of the kids' toy chest. After she had her medicine she seemed in a really good mood. She even played Wii bowling with us. She's not very good at it. She practically fell over a few times, but she sure tried hard.

Anyway, before Billy and my mom came back Mrs. Stand gave me a $50 bill as my pay. I felt like that was way too much money. Especially since she got better and all and really didn't need me that much. But she insisted. I'd actually like to give the money to my mom, because I think she needs it. But I can't figure out how because Mrs. Stand said not to tell anyone we hung out and that it would be our little secret. I kind of felt funny about that.

CHAPTER 5

Trix 'n Treats

Henry VIII was feeling a royal pain. It took all his might not to slam the telephone receiver back into its cradle, but he managed to see the irksome conversation through to its faux polite ending. He simply wouldn't give the caller the satisfaction of knowing she'd rattled him.

"Well again, you enjoy your day. I know it's a favorite time for you," said the maddeningly serene voice on the other end of the line. "And as always, God be with you."

The monarch stayed silent until the connection was safely terminated. Then, through gritted teeth, he signed off. "And Heaven help *you*, you sanctimonious—"

Red-faced and glowering, King Henry opened his door and bellowed into the outer office. "Don't ever put that woman through again!"

"All right! Don't take my head off!" said Mrs. Chapel, who was dressed as Anne Boleyn.

It was Trix 'n Treats Day at Little Fawn Country Day. The school's Halloween celebration was normally a day the headmaster relished. As per longstanding tradition—ah, how he loved tradition!—all faculty and administrators came decked out in full costume. Lower School students did the same, and the day concluded with student and teacher dress parades, complete with prizes, sugar-loaded goodie bags, and a photo shoot by the local newspaper.

Apart from the socially sanctioned opportunity to gorge on sweets, what he loved most about Trix 'n Treats was the opportunity it afforded him to mimic the sartorial splendor of some of history's most intriguing characters. In the past few years he'd come to school outfitted as Napoleon, Nero, and most recently, Achilles. The latter was a Brad Pitt-inspired impersonation, complete with plumed helmet, breastplate, and dagger; for some reason it made several of the younger children cry.

This year he had chosen to recreate the splendid and decorous King Henry, making a regal impression—if he did say so himself—in his tapestry cloak, jacquard shirt, and bejeweled velvet hat. He'd even coaxed Mrs. Chapel into dressing as his infamous second queen, which he'd thought would add to the merriment of it all. But now he wasn't so sure; it was only nine in the morning and already he was tiring of his assistant's seemingly bottomless supply of gallows humor.

Take her head off indeed.

"Mrs. Chapel," he sighed, "I'm in no mood for puns. I'm quite serious. I don't want to speak to anyone from Our Lady of Perpetual Sorrows unless I initiate the call—especially not that insufferable Mother Bernadette. Do you know why she had the audacity to call me?"

"Why, no, I don't," Mrs. Chapel lied, though she had, as usual, surreptitiously listened in on every word of her boss's telephone conversation. ("*Scientia est potentia*," she would later explain under subpoena. "Knowledge is power.")

"She said it was to wish me a happy All Souls' Day. Hah! That alone is a backhanded insult. I know she thinks we're all devil worshippers over here. I bet she can't stand that our 'pagan' parade always gets such magnificent coverage in the *Peninsula Dish*. And just who is *she* to turn her nose up at dressing in costume? I mean, she's *always* in costume. Of all the—"

"Now, now," Mrs. Chapel said, swishing prettily in her gold-brocaded deep emerald gown. "Be nice. I'm sure you're reading into this. Don't let it ruin your day."

"Nice, my foot," he shouted, stomping a square-toed and buckled clog on the floor for emphasis. "The real reason she called was to *let it drop* that two of her OLPS seniors got perfect scores on the October SATs. Perfect!"

Mrs. Chapel feigned surprise, but she already knew why King Henry had his knickers in a knot. None of the students at Country Day had come close to achieving such a feat. Even Chip Luffhauser, acknowledged brain and shoo-in for June's valedictorian slot, had earned only a 2280 out of a possible 2400. Highly respectable, yes; perfect, no. Mother Bernadette, principal of OLPS, did have a way of knowing how and when to rub salt into Dr. Nobler's stigmata.

"Well," he railed on, "it makes no difference to me if a couple of those kids got lucky. No difference at all. Our students are much more...er, creative. And well-rounded."

"Indeed."

"They're not little robots. They're lifelong learners. *Lifelong*, I tell you."

"Yes, Your Majesty."

"Besides, we'll see who has the last laugh. The school year's not over yet, is it?"

"No, Your Majesty."

Unlike the real Anne Boleyn, Mrs. Chapel knew how to calm a tempestuous Tudor down. Her subservience took the edge off her boss's royal pique, at least temporarily.

The headmaster inhaled deeply, which was not easy considering the tightness of his under corset. What would Henry do, he asked himself. WWHD? Of course! He would stay with his battle plan, hone it, refine it.

"Tell Mr. Jakes I want to see him," the king ordered.

Mrs. Chapel nodded toward the doorway where Benjamin Jakes, or Commander Spock, as he preferred to be known on this special day, stood waiting.

"He'd like to see you too, sir."

"Well, speak of the devil," said Nobler.

• • •

Josie winced as she dropped pieces of rolled dough into the deep fryer. The hot oil crackled and spattered. She always reminded herself too late that she ought to wear protective goggles when she made *strufoli*. The path that led to deliciously gooey Italian honey balls was strewn with occupational hazards. Once the fried bits of dough turned golden brown she would have to stir them into a saucepan of boiling honey, and then remove them with a slotted spoon. She'd be coated in drippy goo before the fun part started, but the result was always worth the effort. The sticky concoction, heaped on platters and covered in multicolored sprinkles, was an irresistible treat.

She reached for an oversized plastic container of sprinkles and winced again as she noted the price sticker affixed to its side. She'd sprung for the Halloween novelty assortment of red, orange, and yellow, and like all seasonal culinary items, this jar of jimmies sold at a premium. The cost of all the donations Josie was encouraged to make to Country Day's fundraisers and school events was rapidly adding up, and so far the high-end catering jobs she'd hoped would result from hobnobbing with the school's wealthy parents had not materialized.

She knew that even the wealthy were cutting back in times like these, but she still hoped the upcoming holiday season would be a boon. Meanwhile, she'd just have to forge ahead. These wouldn't be the sprinkles that broke the camel's back.

Besides, no matter how much red ink was showing on Cooler's books, she'd have to put a brave face on things for Torre. Last week she'd found an extra fifty dollars in the store's cash register. After she'd grilled Pete and Jorge about having shortchanged some unfortunate customer, her son had finally confessed to putting his far-too-generous babysitting pay there himself. He shouldn't worry about her finances that way, she'd told him. "Your job is to do well at that school of yours and keep your scholarship, Shortcake. That's the only thing you have to do. *Capeesh?*"

Josie left the *strufoli* to cool and went upstairs to take a shower. She didn't want to be late for the costume parade. Max had told her he was dressing up as a biker, complete with a do-rag, sunglasses, a leather motorcycle vest, and fake tattoos. That she didn't want to miss.

The previous Sunday, a nearly eighty-degree Indian summer interlude, Max and Josie had rented bicycles in Spring Lake and ridden on the boardwalk—a privilege afforded to locals in the off-season. Max had far outdone his original offer of coffee or a drink, bringing along a picnic lunch of corned beef sandwiches on rye, half-sour pickles, coleslaw, and chocolate rugelach. Josie enjoyed the food immensely, as she did with almost all food she didn't have to prepare herself.

She'd enjoyed the company too, despite a warning from Emily that the recently divorced math teacher was still nursing a broken heart. "His wife left him to live in an ashram in India," the seemingly omniscient Emily had explained. "When she came to pack up her things she was wearing an orange robe. *Orange.* She looked like a traffic cone."

As they sat alongside the surf, Max had regaled Josie with behind-the-scenes tales from Little Fawn Country Day, recounting some legendary skirmishes between "Dr. No" and his loyal minions—Mrs. Tripper the English teacher, and Madame Millefleur the French instructor among them—and a small coterie of old-school educators who called themselves "the Resistance." There was an ongoing struggle, he'd explained, between those like himself who believed in teaching a firm foundation of educational basics and those who imagined that reading, writing, and 'rithmetic were quaint and outdated notions. "Last year Dr. No asked the Lower School to throw out the multiplication tables. Said memorization was counterproductive to creativity. Hell, he'd throw out the alphabet if we let him, or at least thirteen of the twenty-six letters! Too many to remember."

Josie had enjoyed the day, even if her date did perhaps tell her a smidgen more than she wanted to know about the shortcomings of her son's benefactor. Dr. Nobler and his school might not be perfect, but Torre was getting the opportunity of a lifetime, and she wasn't about to mess with a proverbial gift horse. Still, there was no denying that Max was fun to be with, and heaven knew she could use some fun.

She took a little extra time with her hair and makeup before packing up her Halloween honey balls.

· · ·

Mrs. Chapel pulled back the hood of her gown, drew out her folding fan, and waved it across her face and neck. *My*, she thought, *they certainly dressed for warmth in the sixteenth century.* Good thing the real Anne Boleyn had never lived long enough to have hot flashes.

She eyed the shut door of the headmaster's office. If she wanted to find out once and for all what Dr. Nobler and Benjamin Jakes were brewing up, she'd have to resort to her old trick of putting her ear to a water glass pressed against the wall. She was sorely tempted to do so, for she was especially curious about all the *tête-à-têtes* between the two men of late. Unable to spot a glass with the ideal diameter, she reached for a coffee mug. She was about to shut her outer office door when her plans were derailed by the arrival of a boisterous kindergarten class in full masquerade mode.

"Miss Markle," she said regally, if a tad edgily, to the children's leader, "to what do we owe this…this *delightful* visit?"

"*Oooh*, who can this be, children?" the teacher queried her flock. "What an interesting dress. Let's see, is this, uh, the Wicked Witch of the West?"

The kindergartners shrieked with laughter at their teacher's guess. "No, no, not her!"

"Well, is it the Good Witch of the North?"

The vote was split this time, with a few of the children tentatively assenting.

"Well, what kind of witch is she then?" Miss Markle pressed on.

A tiny blonde girl outfitted as a sunflower piped up. "She's not a witch. She's a *queeennnn*," she said, making a pretty curtsey. "Like in *Shrek*."

"Oh, I see, a *queeeennn*," echoed Miss Markle.

"Indeed," answered Mrs. Chapel, "and you would be—?" She stopped herself from saying words the kindergartners might repeat to their parents as she eyed Miss Markle's sheer hip-hugging harem pants, midriff-baring top, and veiled fez-like headpiece.

"She's a genie!" shouted several of the kindergartners in gleeful unison.

"Look at the diamond in her tummy!" the sunflower insisted. "Isn't that awesome?"

"It certainly is something," said Mrs. Chapel. She made a mental note to write a Trix 'n Treats dress code memo next year banning, among other things, exposed and bejeweled navels. "Well, again, to what do owe this pleasure?"

"We were just on our way to gym class and I thought we'd say hello to the headmaster. I know how much Dr. Nobler enjoys Halloween, and just look at the wonderful costumes the boys and girls are wearing!"

Mrs. Chapel softened for a moment. Even the most jaded sovereign would have to admit this was an especially cute gaggle of ninjas, mermaids, superheroes, spacemen, and dinosaurs. Dr. Nobler would probably get a special charge out of Lucy and Harry Stand, the sister and brother dressed respectively as a laundry basket and a front-loader washing machine. *Why their mother must be very clever to have come up with those costumes,* thought Mrs. Chapel. But the headmaster never liked being interrupted when he and Jakes were talking about...whatever it was they talked about.

"What a shame," she said. "He's tied up in a meeting right now, I'm afraid. He'll be so sorry to have missed you all, but he's looking forward to seeing you at the parade and the party."

The children seemed just as happy to get on with their journey to the gymnasium. Miss Markle, though, looked a bit crestfallen. She was sorry to miss a private audience with a headmaster who typically grew flustered at the mere sight of her, even when she wasn't in such suggestive regalia. Mrs. Chapel sniffed as she watched the curvaceous genie sashay away. Some people, she reflected, had no shame.

Now, what had she been about to do when she was interrupted? She looked down at her hand and realized she was still clutching an empty coffee mug. Not much time left. Once the next period bell rang, which would be any minute, Benjamin Jakes would have to go back to his classroom. She couldn't risk getting caught blatantly eavesdropping, but of course no one could blame her if she just happened to need something from the file cabinet that abutted the headmaster's office wall. She crouched down, rummaged for a piece of paper in its lowest drawer, and just happened to lean against the wall to steady herself as she did so. From within Dr. Nobler's inner sanctum, she could make out a few garbled words.

"Really think...young man took...?" said the headmaster.

"Opportunity...sure...mother looked at me funny," Jakes answered.

"Hard to swallow, anyway...under your hat...forget...too important."

"I agree, but...if you need leverage..."

"Jakes...you"—Dr. Nobler laughed—"you have a minimal mind."

A *minimal mind?* Or did he say *criminal mind?* Mrs. Chapel leaned in closer to the wall, but it was no use. The end-of-period bell sounded and within moments the two men emerged from the inner office.

"Mrs. Chapel, what are you doing hunkering over there?" Dr. Nobler demanded.

"Just looking for a file, Your Majesty."

"Ah. Well, thanks for stopping by, Benjamin. And Mrs. Chapel, speaking of files, do you have the updates on the Capital Campaign donations from the accountant?"

Mrs. Chapel braced herself. She had already peeked at the tallies. They were good, some would say very good, but they did not keep pace with her boss's spiraling royal-scale desires. She knew the numbers weren't going to do much to improve his mood.

She retrieved a manila envelope from her desk and handed it over. "Here you go," she said without meeting the headmaster's gaze.

Moments later, from behind Dr. Nobler's desk, she could have sworn she heard an utterance that sounded suspiciously like a four letter word. Well, Henry always was a bawdy one.

• • •

As the founder and CEO of Ergo-Geri Inc., Hal Thorn was a man with big plans. He had never sat at the helm of a company before. However, a string of corporate vice presidencies, in which he had to kowtow to lesser men and carry out the grunt work necessitated by their unimaginative visions, had induced in him an insatiable hunger to be the big cheese. Now that he was number one (albeit the only C-level executive or executive of any sort) of his very own company, nothing would stop him from fulfilling his ultimate dream: to make enough money to spend the rest of his life loafing around on a Mexican beach somewhere, like those guys in *The Shawshank Redemption*. (The idea was especially appealing to him because he fancied he looked so much like Tim Robbins.)

The medical supply business was everything he hoped it would be and more. It was only a matter of time, and very little time at that, before his dream came to fruition. In the meanwhile, there was much to be done.

In spite of his many preoccupations, Hal didn't hesitate to answer his phone when he eyed Preston Nobler's number on his caller ID. He and the headmaster went all the way back to their boyhood boarding school days. Their joint study efforts, combined with their mutual belief that the school's honor code was for pussies, ultimately earned them both slots on the Dean's List and acceptances at sufficiently prestigious colleges. Afterward, the boyhood roommates continued an alliance, knowing that each could, if he wished, produce enough irrefutable evidence to cast a permanent blight on the other's reputation.

Besides, Hal reminded himself, Nobler was a chump. And Hal liked chumps.

"Hello, old man. What can I do you for?" he greeted his caller.

"Hal, how are you? Say, have you got a minute?"

"Sure. What's the problem? You sound awful. Isn't this, you know, your favorite day? Who are you dressed as, Alexander the Great? Attila the Hun?"

"Henry VIII."

"Well, that explains it. Are your tights giving you a wedgie?"

The headmaster shuffled in his chair. As a matter of fact, his tights *were* giving him a wedgie, but he had bigger problems at the moment.

"Listen Hal, I've just been looking at the numbers for the Givers of Knowledge campaign."

"Not so hot?"

"How did you know?"

"Listen old man, everyone's holding back a little bit these days. Lydia tells me her girlfriends all want to make a show of being on board but, come on, you know everybody's tight for cash right now."

"It's an investment in their children's future. It's a commitment to excellence. It's…"

Hal suppressed a chortle, covering it up with a fake cough. "'Scuse me," he mumbled. "Allergies." You had to love this fellow, he thought. More often than not he actually believed his own bullshit.

"Well, this level of funding won't do," said Nobler, "and that's the bottom line."

"Just how much are we talking about?"

He named a sum far higher than Hal anticipated. He whistled appreciatively. "*Whew!* Well, I'd say you're doing fine, under the circumstances."

"It's not enough for the soccer stadium I've decided to build, let alone the planetarium. Do you know how much digital projection and full-dome video costs?"

"What are you going to do, buddy? I know you've got more fundraising planned, but you can't get blood from stones."

"Precisely, and that's why I'm calling you. I've got to grow this money, and fast. Tell me more about this IPO you're putting together. What kind of timetable are we talking about?"

Hal's expensively crafted jaw dropped and he found himself momentarily speechless. Had this actually just fallen into his lap? Yes! And why not? He'd always sensed he was born under a lucky star, that he was somehow special. He fake-coughed again as he quickly regrouped and geared up for his well-honed pitch.

In the end, Hal thought, it had been as easy as taking candy from a baby. No, strike that. It was as easy as taking Halloween treats from a grown man prancing around as Henry VIII.

"Zihuatanejo, here I come," breathed Hal.

On the other end of the line, Mrs. Chapel also exhaled as she ever so gently replaced the receiver of her desk phone into its cradle. She'd never cared for the preening, overbearing Hal Thorn much, and might have been surprised to know that she shared with him a similar goal of a laid back early retirement. Maybe she would be running that bed-and-breakfast in Vermont and writing screenplays in her spare time sooner rather than later. She hoped there would be time during the afternoon's festivities to call her broker and see if he knew how to get in on the ground floor of Ergo-Geri's IPO.

• • •

The Peninsula Dish: All the Scoops Along the Shore

November 1 edition

COUNTRY DAY CELEBRATES HALLOWEEN IN STYLE

(LITTLE FAWN) In their annual and much beloved "Trix 'n Treats" Halloween parade, tykes and teachers at Little Fawn Country Day yesterday wowed parents and guests with an array of creative costumes. After the promenade, Grand Marshall Henry VIII, a.k.a. headmaster Preston Nobler, awarded prizes for most creative ensemble to English teacher Francine Tripper, who came as a colon; and French teacher Maxine Millefleur who, while masquerading as a fetching Marie Antoinette, distributed candy to dazzled onlookers and cleverly jested, "Let them eat Kit Kats."

Dr. Nobler went on to explain that in keeping with his pedagogical philosophy of relentless self-esteem boosting, all of the children would receive prizes. However, if you ask us, top honors, had they been awarded, ought to have gone to five-year-old strawberry-locked cuties Lucy and Harry Stand, scions of the Jersey shore's favorite son, Billy Stand. The diminutive duo came teamed as a laundry basket and clothes washer.

(*Pssst*...don't tell anyone, but we have it on good authority that a certain genie, a.k.a. dedicated kindergarten educator Marisa Markle, was the mastermind behind the ingenious ensembles.)

After the prizes, local chanteuse Mindy Battin, Country Day seventh grader, gave the children a fright with her rendition of "If You Go into the Woods Tonight." Awesome job, Miss Mindy. Your song truly gave us chills.

Kudos also to LFCD's Hospitality Committee: Celeste Battin, Lydia Thorn, and chairwoman Emily Luffhauser. Their refreshment assortment was delightful. We especially enjoyed the Luffhauser Farms hot apple cider. Ditto some delightful Italian honey balls, provided by a local vendor.

Speaking of Emily Luffhauser, is there any truth to the rumor that she is cooking something up with Billy Stand—perhaps something to benefit her pet cause, the Wild Bay Food Bank? Stay tuned.

More parade photos, page 6.

• • •

Language Arts Journal, November 1 Mindy Battin

Last night turned out pretty interesting, even though <u>I feel I am too old to dress up for Halloween anymore</u>. My Mom and I took my little brother Lars trick or treating. He was dressed as a pirate, which <u>I feel is not so lame if you're a first grader like he is</u>.

We drove Lars to Billy Stand's house because we all wanted to see what kind of treats they were handing out there. Billy's house has a big gate but it was open and there was a line of kids there, so we knew they were giving out good stuff. I walked Lars to the front door and sure enough he got a movie-sized box of Milk Duds. But it was just some boring housekeeper type lady giving out the candy. Then this morning I found out that Billy took his twins out trick or treating to a few places himself. Even to Torre's mom's store! <u>I feel really, really bad we missed that.</u>

But like I said things still turned out interesting. When me and Lars got back in the car I saw my Mom try to sneak her hand into the pillowcase Lars was collecting candy in. She thinks I don't see her sneaking cookies and candy and stuff but I do. I see lots of things.

Anyway when Mom was trying to get her hand in the bag she pressed down on our garage door opener by mistake. And she didn't notice it but I saw one of Billy's garage doors go up. It's like we have our own secret key to Billy's house. <u>I feel like that is really interesting</u>.

CHAPTER 6:

Thanksgiving Feast

Emily stood in the empty lot behind the Wild Bay Food Bank, where an impromptu game of student-versus-faculty touch football was underway. She looked at all she had created, and she saw it was good.

Thanksgiving turned out to be yet another of those balmy, brilliant days that the local weatherman insisted on branding as "unseasonably warm," yet this autumn had been chockablock with just such climatic jewels. In fact, Emily realized with a bit of a start, she could not remember such a glorious stretch since the fall of 2001. In those weeks after the towers fell—an event many on the peninsula had witnessed firsthand and from which some had never returned—the shimmering sun and soft breezes had been glaring incongruities. Emily shuddered briefly, recalling how the weather gods had mocked them as they'd gone about their daily lives in a daze. Then, for the briefest of moments, she registered a fleeting whiff of foreboding. Just as quickly, though, she shook it off.

Hell with that, she thought. No time for any negative sentiments, ever. She was a Luffhauser, albeit by marriage. That meant there was always something constructive she could do—just as she was today, at the Wild Bay Food Bank Holiday Feast.

Four hundred and twenty-three dinners had been served inside the food bank over the past four hours. Four hundred and twenty-three needy residents of Wild Bay—children, seniors, entire families who had nowhere else to go—had enjoyed a lavish array of smoked turkey, roasted yams, sautéed collards with bacon bits, baby carrots in brown sugar, and vats of Emily's dear friend Josie's Italian sausage stuffing. And who had served it to them? Who had foregone their own Thanksgiving feasts in order to minister to those less fortunate? None other than the selfless parents, students, and faculty of Little Fawn Country Day joined by—wait for it—Billy and MaryAnn Stand, and that terribly sweet black man, Moses Jones.

It had all been Emily's doing, she reminded herself with immense satisfaction (with a little help from her friends, of course, but still). She was the one who had coaxed Billy to give the intimate $500 per ticket benefit concert at the Sea Wall. And that concert had raised the funds for this charitable event—not to mention yielding a healthy surplus that would jump-start her future plans for the food bank's expansion onto the adjoining lot on which she now stood. Of course the concert sold out within hours of its announcement, with the bulk of the ticket-holders being FOLs (Friends of the Luffhausers), many of the Country Day set among them. Emily was the one who organized the Thanksgiving food purchase (though some vendors, like dear Josie, could always be called upon to donate). She had publicized the free dinner in the *Peninsula Dish* and the *Wild Bay Press* (and she did look fabulous in that photo with Billy and Moses, if she did say so herself).

To even her own surprise, Emily had finally been able to talk the initially resistant Dr. Nobler into making the Wild Bay Food Bank Feast a school-wide cause. Nobler was, in Emily's humble opinion, the small-minded sort who thought of everything in life as a zero-sum game. The more disposable income funneled into one cause, like feeding the hungry, the less available for another, like turning a school into a—what was he calling it lately?—Maxi-Versatile Multi-Media-Enabled Sports, Science, and Humanities Lifelong Learning Complex. But he had decided to jump on board her philanthropic train. He'd bought tickets to the concert for himself and his mother Dorothy, who belied her eighty-seven years by swaying, clapping, and stomping as heartily as anyone in the packed house. He'd even announced that students who volunteered to help cook and serve at the Food Bank Feast would accrue school service hours toward their mandatory yearly total.

Emily wasn't certain why the headmaster had acted so benevolently. Possibly her irresistible charm had worn him down, though even she had to admit this wasn't likely. The fact was he seemed to be in a better mood than usual since Halloween, though she was not sure why. He was almost acting like a man who'd won the lottery.

Oh well, no matter; the result was all that counted. The day was going splendidly, and the *pièce de résistance*—the Luffhauser Farms pumpkin pie à la mode, which was sure to win her even more accolades—was still ahead.

Suddenly the crowd of students, parents, teachers, and dinner guests watching the ad hoc football game erupted into a roar. Placing her hand across her brow to shield against the glare of the sun's late afternoon angle, Emily watched with delight as her eldest son Chip completed a long, high pass to Moses Jones, who went on to run the ball across the faculty's goal line for a winning touchdown. Max, in hot pursuit (or what passed as hot pursuit for a lightly paunchy middle-aged math teacher), gave up his futile attempt to tag the receiver and threw up his hands in mock exasperation. "That's why they call him The Magnet," he said of Moses.

It was true. Back in the day when he'd been a star wide receiver for Rutgers, his worshipful fans had dubbed Moses with the sporting sobriquet "The Magnet". It was an acknowledgement of the fact that even when his quarterback's pass had come off wild and wobbly, the football seemed to fly across the field straight for his super-charged hands. It was as though the ball and his hands were destined to meet, and once the ball was in his possession there was no stopping him. It had not been unusual for the massive yet fleet-footed Magnet to run forty, fifty, even seventy yards, shaking off his would-be tacklers like so many pesky gnats. Years later, with the second of his legendary careers still in full swing, Moses seemed as skilled and agile as ever on the field. It seemed for all the world that, if he so chose, he could put down his saxophone, put on his cleats, and pick up where he'd left off.

And such a nice man, thought Emily. *So polite, and so generous.* Emily had been as startled as everyone else—including, apparently, Billy Stand himself—when Moses had walked onto the Sea Wall's small stage, sax in hand, at the benefit concert a few days before. The two old friends had embraced for a long moment before Moses started in on the intro to the old C-Side Band classic, *Jughandle Head-On.* The song was about a fateful prom night car crash in which a golden boy prom king is decapitated in the pounding rain when he mistakes a Route 18 entrance ramp for an exit. The perennial Jersey crowd-pleaser—for who among the Garden State's native sons and daughters had not nearly fallen prey to the same tragic misperception?—ripped the lid off what had been a fairly mellow acoustical evening. The Sea Wall, stuffed well past its legal maximum occupancy with Country Day parents up way past their bedtimes, had literally shaken as baby boomers and Gen X-ers alike leapt from their seats and broke into what could actually pass for a semblance of dance—although not before stopping to text their kids' babysitters to warn them they'd be late.

How Moses had known about the benefit concert Emily wasn't certain, but with the preternatural aplomb of someone for whom things invariably tended to work out, she'd simply accepted his materialization as the hand of Providence giving her its usual shove in the right direction. She had no way of knowing that Billy's former bandmate had been summoned via a 3 a.m. phone call from MaryAnn, pleading with him to help save her marriage.

• • •

Moses and MaryAnn had known one another since the moment Philly Yo had introduced Moses and Billy. It was a moment that, like so many things about Billy and his band, had become firmly lodged in the lore of pop music.

Along with recently recruited band members Danny Krakowski and Tony Bonodaro, MaryAnn and Billy had been hanging out on the stage of the Sea Wall when the six-foot-four, 250-pound Moses strode in. No formal introduction was needed, as The Magnet's face and physique were familiar enough sights to Scarlet Knights fans across the state. In any case, there would have been no time for pleasantries, for at the instant Moses reached out his massive hand to shake Billy's, a precariously hung fifty-amp three-way splitter fell loose from its overhead rigging. Utilizing the instincts that had earned him his athletic fame, Moses reached out and caught the stage light in the nanosecond before it would have crashed directly into Billy's skull.

"Can I try out for your band?" Moses asked Billy.

"What do *you* think?" Billy laughed.

Within the hour, MaryAnn and Philly became the first two people on earth to hear Billy, Danny, Tony, and Moses make music together. MaryAnn had watched with a mixture of joy and sadness as she realized with utter certainty that Billy would soon be going places where she might not be able to follow. Yet she never begrudged Moses for being the tipping point that took the C-Side Band into a new and transcendent realm.

On the contrary, the slight, freckled strawberry blonde and the colossal scalp-shaven African-American became fast friends. They recognized and appreciated in one another two shared qualities: an intense loyalty to Billy and an equally intense intellect. Moses, whose 4.0 grade point average had been something of an anomaly among college football players, was tired of, as his sainted grandmother used to say, hiding his light under a bushel so he'd fit in with the jock crowd. Along with playing football and playing the sax, the thing he'd always loved most of all was reading. In MaryAnn, the honor student at the top of her class, Moses found a kindred spirit with whom to talk about Herman Hesse, Virginia Woolf, and Ralph Ellison. On Sundays while Billy, Danny, and Tony hit the surf at Seven Presidents' Beach, MaryAnn and Moses, having discovered a shared penchant for *The New York Times* crossword puzzle, sat on the sand scribbling answers in pen.

When Billy and MaryAnn had broken up, Moses was nearly as distraught as Billy. He missed not only the earnest, clever, down-to-earth girl, but also the grounded, humble qualities she brought out in Billy. Without her, Billy seemed restless and adrift.

When Billy and MaryAnn reunited so many years later, it seemed only natural that they'd asked Moses, now himself married with a brood of children, to be their best man. He'd done the honors with pleasure, as he did when he was asked to become Lucy and Harry's godfather a year later.

So when MaryAnn had called him a week ago, sobbing and strangely slurry in the middle of the night, Moses felt like he had on those rare occasions when he was brought down by an opposing lineman: breathless, confounded, and wondering how the hell this had happened. What was Billy doing to blow it with MaryAnn this time? He was sure as hell going to find out.

The morning after MaryAnn's call, Moses had talked things over with his wife, Delia. The Joneses led a quiet life in Saratoga Springs, New York, where Moses produced albums in a state of the art home recording studio and Delia taught Comparative Literature at Skidmore. They had six children, ages two to thirteen. Neither one could bear the thought of the Stand family unraveling. Delia said she couldn't get away mid-semester, even if she could have found a sitter on short notice, but both agreed it would be a good idea if Moses paid the Stands a visit.

When Moses called MaryAnn back, she told him about Billy's benefit concert that was taking place that very night. Moses hatched his plan for his surprise entrance. No time like the present, he thought. Fortunately, Saratoga Springs was only three and a half hours from the Jersey shore. More like three if you had a lead foot, which Moses did. He learned a long time ago that any cop who pulled him over would end up letting him go in exchange for an autograph. Even those who didn't recognize his face would know the name on his license, especially once he crossed over the Jersey border.

Moses had been staying with the Stands for the past several days, but when Delia called him to ask how things were, the only answer he could give her was, "Weird." Billy and MaryAnn both seemed genuinely happy to see him, and the three had stayed up long into the nights reminiscing about old times. Moses knew there was a proverbial elephant in the room, but husband and wife seemed determined to ignore it, at least when they were all together. Moses had tried to find a way to broach the subject with Billy as gently as he could when he and his friend were alone.

"So," he'd asked Billy, "how's New Jersey treating you guys?"

"Good," said Billy. "Real fine."

"The kids happy?"

"Man, you see how they are. They're great. They love kindergarten. Love their teacher."

"And MaryAnn? She likes it better back here than in California?"

"Well...yeah. She always wanted to come back home. She always used to say she felt like the ocean was on the wrong side out there—me too, in a way. You know, the sun ought to rise over the ocean, not set over it. Seems more natural somehow. But..." He'd trailed off.

"But what, man?"

"I don't know. I don't know, I thought...well, I thought she'd get more involved back here—go out more—but she has this aversion to crowds or something. It's only getting worse. She just doesn't like being in public. She doesn't even like going to school events, and God knows there are enough of them. Even when I can talk her into going, she bags out early. A while ago she just up and left a dinner there. Just walked on home. It was kinda, you know, embarrassing. I just don't get it."

"Well, she's always been shy, Billy. You know that."

"I know, and trust me, I know that damn song I wrote about her always made matters worse. She's beyond sick of hearing about those damned patent leather shoes. Hell, I'd take it back if could, even if it changed everything that happened with the band. But I don't know how to build a time machine."

"Come on Billy, cut it out. You were a kid. We all were. You think that really bothers her?"

"I dunno. She won't say so. Won't say anything's the matter, but I know there is. I wish she'd make some friends around here. I thought she'd find some girlfriends, maybe other moms, but she says she wants to be home with the kids, that they'll grow up fast and she doesn't want to miss anything. But then…"

"Yeah?"

"Well, she says she doesn't feel well some of the time, but she won't get a checkup or anything. Just says any mother of twins gets tired."

Moses recalled the slurred sound of MaryAnn's voice on the phone. If he didn't know better he would have sworn MaryAnn was drunk, but he'd never known her to drink at all. Not even a beer. He couldn't imagine sharing his odd notion with Billy, at least not yet.

"Maybe," he ventured, "maybe she ought to talk to someone. You know, someone professional."

Billy had only smiled. "I told her that. I asked if she wanted to see a counselor or something, but she just got mad. I'm not sure what to do. But hey, she seems great now that you're around. Can you stick around for a few more days? It feels like she's coming out of her shell with you here."

Moses had agreed to stay through Thanksgiving. He'd known it was the right thing to do. He'd phoned Delia and she'd agreed to put off their family dinner until later in the weekend. Sure enough, with Moses's help, Billy had coaxed MaryAnn into attending the Food Bank Feast. Just before they'd left the house, though, MaryAnn had pulled Moses aside and made a request.

"Moses," she'd said, "can you do me a favor? Can you just keep an eye on Billy today? I have a strange feeling that he—"

Her upper lip had begun to quiver.

"He what?"

"It's crazy—I know you'll say it's crazy—but I just have this feeling there might be, I don't know, someone else."

"Someone else?"

"You know, a girl."

Moses shook his head. "MaryAnn, come on. You know he's not like that. What's gotten into you?"

"Well maybe I'm nuts, like I said—God, I hope I am—but a woman sometimes just has a sixth sense about these things."

Moses had wrapped MaryAnn in a bear hug and patted her strawberry hair. "Honey, I know you're just imagining things, but The Magnet will keep his eyes open for you."

He was true to his word. His days as a wide receiver had honed his instincts for scoping out exactly which players were on the field and what they were doing. He'd stayed alert throughout the Thanksgiving feast, but so far nothing unusual had caught his attention.

Of course, it was a little difficult to keep the big picture in focus. The mothers of Country Day were determined to chat with him. That platinum blonde, the one with the surgically enhanced chest he was trying not to notice, kept trying to tell him about how she couldn't wait for him to hear her daughter Mindy sing "Tis a Gift to Be Simple," accompanying herself on acoustic guitar, at today's after dinner entertainment. Then there was the lady who kept wanting to know what he thought about the football team at Brown, which was evidently the college her daughter planned to attend. And of course there was the energetic Emily, who could not thank him enough—though he ardently tried to get her to stop—for giving so generously of his time.

Then there was that headmaster dude. Dr. Nobler had planted himself beside Moses in the serving line earlier in the day and, having discovered that the Joneses had six children, had been kind enough to offer a detailed history of Little Fawn Country Day and its laudable traditions. Should it turn out that Moses missed New Jersey, Country Day would be happy—*thrilled,* in fact—to embrace his offspring in its fold of lifelong learners.

Moses had had enough of that. A master of evasion on the football field, he managed to sidestep Nobler as the Country Day crowd made its way back inside the Food Bank to dole out pie. Cutting off any possibility that the headmaster might blindside him, Moses sauntered up beside Chip and gave him an avuncular clap across the back.

"You got game, friend," he said.

"Me? Hey, thanks. But I just got lucky out there," said Chip.

"No, really, you've got an arm. You gonna play in college?"

"Mom says no. Says I've got to focus on academics. Besides, I kind of checked it out and Harvard doesn't need any more quarterbacks this year."

"Harvard? Well, I guess you're gonna be busy enough hitting the books."

"So they tell me. Hey, but listen, it was great to play with you today, Magne—er, I mean Mr. Jones."

"How about Moses?"

"Sure. Moses. Thanks again, I really mean it. It was an awesome day."

Moses agreed. It really had been a nice day, but he still needed to figure out if there was any subtext where Billy was concerned. Once the pie had been served, he made it a point to scope out the situation with added vigilance. MaryAnn actually seemed to be enjoying herself. In fact, she and the twins had spent most of the day talking with that perky kindergarten teacher—what was her name?—Miss Markle.

And Billy? Billy was, as always, a favorite with the ladies. The moms spent even more time vying for his attention than they had for Moses's. But, come to think of it, that woman Billy was talking to right now—that Josie that he'd mentioned he knew from his old neighborhood—they did seem awfully friendly. Awfully. But that didn't necessarily mean anything. Did it? Besides, Billy said she used to be his babysitter. So, no way. Right?

Moses closed his eyes and rubbed his temples. He felt distinctly out of his league. At least on a football field, you knew who was on which side. The truth was he didn't know much more about what was going on with Billy and MaryAnn than he had before he'd come to visit.

He knew he'd see the Stands again early in the New Year, though. Moses was scheduled to come back to his home state in January so that he could be honored at a ceremony inducting him into the New Jersey Hall of Fame. Maybe things would straighten themselves out by then. He sent up a silent prayer to that effect, and made a mental pledge to do so every night from then on. Meanwhile, he'd be happy to head home tomorrow to see his big, uncomplicated family.

• • •

The sun set on Thanksgiving Day, with many having much for which to be grateful. In Wild Bay, four hundred and twenty-three men, women, and children gave thanks for the delicious meal they had been offered, though they did not know what tomorrow would bring. In Little Fawn, Emily gave thanks for her success, and stayed up long into the night sketching plans to expand the food bank structure. Celeste, who'd managed to abscond with a leftover pumpkin pie, ate the entire thing—one guilty, frustrated, luscious forkful at a time—and gave thanks that no one caught her in the act. Chip tossed and turned as he thought about the way Persephone's hair had glistened in the sunlight that afternoon, and counted among his many blessings the fact that he saw her smile and cheer as he'd completed his game-winning pass.

As for Persephone, she gave thanks that she would learn about her early admission to Brown in less than three weeks. She carefully lifted from her purse the napkin containing food she had scraped off her plate and hidden away while no one was watching, to make it look as though she'd eaten some dinner. She threw it down the garbage disposal. She was starving, but she'd vowed to eat as little as possible until her college decision was in. Surely the universe would reward such a sacrifice.

• • •

November 30
FROM: Dr. Preston Nobler
TO: All Faculty and Administrative Staff
RE: Diversity! Diversity! Diversity!

It has recently occurred to me that our coming expansion will afford us yet another significant opportunity, i.e. the opportunity to diversify our student body by recruiting children of all ethnic and racial persuasions. I am therefore seeking volunteers to lead an outreach effort to surrounding communities.

This elite team, which shall henceforth be known as the Country Day Rainbow Recruiters (CDRR), will be responsible for identifying suitable minority student candidates, acquainting them and their families with our exceptional academic programs, and shepherding them through our admissions process.

Those interested in joining our Rainbow Recruiters, kindly contact me or Mrs. Chapel as soon as possible. Needless to say, I expect a high level of participation. Let's make a rainbow together!

CHAPTER 7:

Casino Night

Gambling on the Future

The Little Fawn Country Day Hospitality Committee
and Dr. Preston Nobler cordially invite you to a

Vegas Casino Night
Holiday Gala

Please join us for a night of fine food and games
at the Little Fawn Country Club on Friday, December 15
from 7 p.m. to midnight.

Tickets: $250 per person
(includes $50 worth of gambling chips!)
All proceeds to benefit the
Givers of Knowledge Capital Campaign

(And remember, what happens at Casino Night stays
at Casino Night!)

Dress: Black tie

"*God damn it.*" Preston Nobler sucked in his stomach and zipped up the fly of his tuxedo pants. He exhaled as he fastened his cummerbund. His mother had been right as usual; this get-up couldn't be let out any more. He would simply have to spring for a new one if he was going to plan more formal fundraisers, which he most certainly was. But tonight, he would have to suck it up—and in. He wondered if it was possible to damage an internal organ this way—maybe a spleen or something.

"*God damn it,*" he muttered again. This was turning out to be a hell of a day.

If the good Lord were counting, He would have known it was the fifteenth—no, sixteenth—time he had taken His name in vain since early afternoon. Nobler had let the first fourteen epithets fly as he'd reviewed the results of the Little Fawn Country Day seniors' Early Decision college admissions results: one epithet for each prestigious school that had deferred—or worse, outright rejected—one of his students.

Dartmouth, Penn, Columbia, Duke, Amherst, Wesleyan, Williams, Tufts, Hopkins, Colgate, and Vanderbilt had each passed up a chance to snag a Little Fawn lifelong learner in the first round of applications. Brown had deferred *three*, including legacy applicant Persephone Thorn, prolonging the kids' anxious misery until the first of April.

Mrs. Chapel had warned him that perhaps the night of Early Decision results was a bad time to plan a fundraiser. "*Caveat cupiditas,*" she'd said. "Beware your ambition." But had he listened? Of course not. Why should he have? He had been on a roll. Hal had assured him that the IPO in which he'd covertly invested Country Day's GOK funds was going to be more lucrative than he'd dared to hope. He'd had an enthusiastic response to his Rainbow Recruiters initiative, too, and Mr. Jakes was making progress with his special project. The headmaster had brooked no thought that the universe would turn against him in the midst of such carefully crafted success.

Friggin' universe.

Now he'd have to face a horde of angry senior class parents. As far as they were concerned, their children's dashed academic hopes were the result not of any shortcomings on their part, but rather of Country Day's diminishing reputation among college admissions officers. They'd want to harangue him about the school's statewide rankings and standardized test scores all night. They'd threaten subtly, or not so subtly, to transfer their younger children to that cursed OLPS. They'd—they'd—

Wait. He had an idea. *It's a bit of risk, but…no, this could work.*

Taking what tiny steps the constriction of his pants would allow, he hunted down his cell phone and speed dialed Emily, who he knew would be at the Little Fawn Country Club attending to last minute details.

"Emily, it's Preston," he said. "Say, you know what? Let's change the cash bar to an open bar."

• • •

Lydia walked through her closet, feeling utterly assaulted by its racks of festive prints and perky pastels. She reached for a strapless black sheath. The color reflected her mortification, and she grimly shimmied into it. *Deferred!* What a miserable choice of word. Her own alma mater had *deferred* her daughter. What were they thinking? Why, Brown would be lucky to have Persephone. Any college would. Hell, Lydia was almost ready to consider Cornell, though in the end she shuddered at the thought, briskly rubbing her exposed shoulders.

To make matters worse, Lydia had given in to the temptation to call a friend whose daughter was a senior at Our Lady of Perpetual Sorrows.

"Accepted Early Action to Georgetown," her friend had informed her, trying with all her might to suppress her giddiness. It turned out OLPS also had a number of its seniors accepted into early placements at Yale, Stanford, MIT, Notre Dame, and many of the very institutions that had turned up their noses at Country Day students.

Emerging from her closet, Lydia gave herself a once-over in her mirror. "I wonder what that jackass Nobler has to say for himself?" she said to Hal, who stood deftly arranging his bow tie.

"Now, Lydia, relax. Everything will turn out okay."

She sighed. Hal had been so busy with his IPO that he had barely registered the excruciating rituals of college admission that had consumed his wife and daughter of late. "Can't we just buy an essay?" he'd asked, as Lydia and Persephone had agonized over the relative merits of various topics: Most Memorable Person, Most Influential Book, or Adversity You've Overcome. But Lydia knew her husband's suggestion was not only unethical but also impractical. Colleges could smell professional intervention a mile away, she'd read in various guides that purported to know the ins and outs of the process. And so she'd had no choice but to pen the essay, "My Battle with My Overbite", on her daughter's behalf.

Even now, Hal insisted on being blithely optimistic. "Come on," he said, "Persey will be admitted later. I'm sure it's just a demographics thing. Too many kids from upscale zip codes applied early. The Ivies have to reach out to the underprivileged first. Sew up some Pell grants. It's good public relations.

"Anyway," he added, coming up behind his wife, "this will make you feel better." He slipped his hand into his pocket and pulled out a little blue box.

Lydia couldn't help but smile. It was undeniably true; such boxes always goosed her spirits. She gently lifted its cover and smiled up at her husband as he fastened the platinum and diamond Tiffany garden dragonfly pendant around her neck.

"Something to remember me by," he said, and Lydia laughed at his silly little joke. By the time the couple pulled out of their driveway and waved good-bye to their daughter, she felt almost herself again. Besides, Lydia consoled herself, Persey was taking the deferral news rather well. In fact, she seemed remarkably unperturbed, and insisted she was looking forward to a relaxing night downloading Netflix and ordering in a pizza.

The Thorns passed the Peninsula Pie Pizza delivery van on their way out, and Lydia flagged down its driver so that Hal could pay and tip him. Neither parent, of course, could have known that their daughter would feed the pepperoni pie to the family's two Cavalier King Charles Spaniels, piece by double cheese piece.

• • •

Josie did not consider herself a criminally minded person. Surely tucking an inventory control tag inside your cocktail dress so that you could return the garment to Nordstrom's later didn't count as breaking an actual law. Did it? She shouldn't even have to carry it on her conscience as a venal sin, she reasoned, because she was already paying penance. The plastic security panel, tucked through the side zipper of her beaded navy blue silk chiffon, dug into her midriff. She quickly unzipped, placed a Band-Aid over the spot to ameliorate the chafing, and tucked in the tag again. She had chosen her outfit carefully; the dress's matching jacket would cover the small bulge the tag created. Maybe she did have at least a potentially successful criminal mind, she thought.

Nah. If she did, she reminded herself, she wouldn't be so strapped for funds. As things stood, Josie was just covering necessities. Extras like fancy dresses for these school soirées were out of the question. Cooler at the Shore was doing a reasonably brisk business day to day, but she still hadn't reaped the alleged catering bonanza Emily kept insinuating would come her way so long as she continued to promote herself by donating fare to this seemingly endless parade of events.

Josie was "doing her part," in Emily-speak, again tonight by donating a basket on which casino players could use their "winnings" to bid. It was a compilation of gourmet Italian foods: a large tin of extra virgin olive oil, a sleeve of prosciutto de Parma, a wedge of Reggiano parmesan, packages of truffle tortellini and squid ink linguini, and an array of Toblerone and Baci chocolates. But the real draw, or so Emily had assured her, was a gift certificate for an in-home catered dinner party for six. "Give someone a taste and I'm sure they'll be your loyal customers for life," Emily had said. From her lips to God's ears, Josie thought—which, knowing Emily, she dared hope just might be the way things worked.

• • •

Emily stood Zen-still amidst the frenetic whirl of preparations at the Little Fawn Country Club. For all her outward serenity, her keen eyes missed no detail. The Casino Night professional party crew was busy hanging wall coverings and light fixtures that would transform the club's stately décor into what the party planner had assured her would be, in his words, "a glitzapalooza."

The crew hauled in a gaggle of slot machines and a giant roulette wheel, and set up tables for blackjack, poker, and craps. They stocked the cashier's station with colored chips of various denominations, and with Basket Booty Dollars for which the chips could be redeemed. The idea was that guests would (quickly) gamble away their fifty dollars' worth of "complimentary" chips, purchase more with real cash, and use their winnings of Basket Booty Dollars to bid on donated goods and services. Casino Night fundraisers were basically gift basket auctions with an adrenaline-pumping twist. Emily, an aficionado in such matters, knew you had to keep things fresh if you were overseeing a long money-sucking campaign.

A few minutes earlier she had hung up with Dr. Nobler and conveyed to the country club manager the headmaster's desire to switch from a pay-as-you-go cash bar to an open bar for the evening. The manager was happy to oblige, for everyone knew that open bar tabs paid by the host ultimately meant much more money for the house. For a moment, Emily had thought to counsel Dr. Nobler about that, but her keen mind swiftly evaluated all the variables and she held her tongue. Vices tended to cluster, and more freely flowing liquor would likely translate into an increased appetite for gambling. Hence, the more chip purchases, the more "winnings" and higher bids on Booty Baskets.

All in all, the open bar seemed a wise investment, though she knew the headmaster's motivation was, for once, not all about the bottom line. He wanted to mollify all those disappointed senior parents by lubricating them with alcohol. Emily wondered if that might backfire on him, but that part was not her problem. She had no personal bone to pick with Dr. Nobler...at the moment. Her son Chip wouldn't apply to his school of choice until the regular decision cycle. There was no rush. The notion that Harvard wouldn't accept her boy was, well, frankly preposterous. *Wasn't it?*

Stop it, she scolded herself. *Always focus on the positive.* And indeed there was much to be positive about. The club was looking very much like a casino by now, and the bartenders were frantically whipping up pitchers of exotic cocktails. At the front of the room, the staff was setting up a small stage for Billy Stand, who Emily had prevailed upon to honor them with one special song tonight. It was, of course, his classic, "Dealer's Choice," a foot stomper about a working class hero who spends his entire paycheck in Atlantic City every Friday night because it's the only way he can see the beautiful croupier he loves from afar.

Best of all, Billy's song would be the only singing performance of the evening. Casino Night was an adults-only affair, and little Mindy was effectively banished.

Ah, there was Billy now—alone again, from the looks of things.

•   •   •

The blend of ingredients in a Sand Flea—orange rum, apricot brandy, Cointreau, grenadine, and equal parts orange juice and sour mix—turned out to be highly appealing to a large number of partygoers. Several of them burst into empathic tears at Billy's song in which the hero beats the house odds, wins twenty grand, and gets the girl, only to fall to his death through some loose slats in the Atlantic City boardwalk.

Celeste preferred to imbibe Vegas BJs: Jagermeister, banana liqueur, citrus rum, orange juice, and pineapple juice. The mix was, many would later conclude, at least partially responsible for her impromptu pole dance, in which she enlisted a handsome young waiter as the pole.

Giving in once again to her entrenched preference for pastels, Lydia enjoyed an impressive number of Pink Missiles: grapefruit vodka, black raspberry liqueur, grenadine, cranberry juice, grapefruit juice, and ginger ale. With each successive refreshment, she became more philosophical about Persephone's temporary confinement to college admissions limbo. Purchasing a copious number of chips, she tried her luck at the craps table, asserting her newfound philosophy that "life was all a roll of the dice."

Marisa, her diminutive hourglass figure shrink-wrapped in a plunge-neck, sequined Versace knockoff, sipped more than a few Saketinis—simple concoctions of vodka and sake—happy to be free from the curious gazes of kindergarteners for the evening. She sucked the olives slowly and reflectively. Tonight, she vowed, she would make her move. She noted with satisfaction that Billy was hanging out at the bar knocking back a beer or two, which ought to make things easier.

Of course, not everyone at Casino Night indulged quite so freely in complimentary cocktails. Aware that his open bar brainstorm had allowed him to dodge a bullet, the headmaster nevertheless thought it wise to keep his guard up. Besides, his mother, once again his date for the festivities, was a formidable teetotaler (although Dorothy did not attack the bar with a hatchet, Carrie Nation-style, her son would have bet real money that the thought crossed her mind).

Also abstemious, for he never drank when he was working, Hal recognized yet another heaven-sent opportunity to promote his IPO. He held a glass of club soda as he trolled the crowd for those whose get-rich-quick impulses might not be sated by the evening's amateur gaming.

Emily stood firm in her determination to never lose control or—God forbid—make a scene. Nursing a watered down gimlet, she resolutely kept her head about her as she presided efficiently over the event, making certain that the food, the entertainment, the gambling, and the auction proceeded in as orderly a fashion as possible.

From a fundraising standpoint, the evening was a substantial success. By the time the Booty Baskets were offered, most of the guests had long blown through their meager complimentary chip allotment and had gleefully purchased handfuls more. When it came time for the Booty Baskets, the bidding was lively. Some—Dorothy Nobler for one—might have said too lively, as when Celeste loudly lamented the fact that none of the baskets contained the sort of things women really desired, "like a coupon for Tantric sex with Sting."

Despite Celeste's quibble, gamblers waving fists full of faux currency were eager to swap it—for what else could they do with it?—for baskets containing everything from an impressive array of Le Creuset cookware donated by Little Fawn's Upper Crust Gourmet, to a darling wee juniper bonsai from the Navesink Nursery, to a top-ten fiction bestseller basket from the Riverside Readers bookstore. The two most sought after items, as it turned out, were a basket from Peninsula Pets offering a redeemable certificate for a Shih Tzu puppy (ultimately won by high bidder Celeste, who vowed to name the dog Sting) and Josie's basket of foodstuffs, complete with her free catering voucher.

Josie watched with mixed feelings as the shout-outs for her prize incited a lively bidding war. For one thing, gambling, even at this level, made her uncomfortable—it always reminded her of Sal's self-destructive streak—and she had declined her own fifty dollars' worth of complimentary tickets. For another thing, she worried about what she had gotten herself into. The frenzy over her donation was all very flattering, but would catering a dinner party for free actually result in getting her any paying jobs?

Not much of a drinker under normal circumstances, she accepted eagerly when her date Max lifted a glass of red wine from a tray offered by a passing waitress. When Hal and Lydia won her Booty Basket and excitedly rushed to request her catering services on New Year's Eve, she downed the entire glass in two gulps and then gamely agreed. *Might as well get it over with.* She felt her face flush and reached for Max to steady herself.

Poor Max, she thought. He'd probably wanted to ask her out for New Year's Eve, but maybe this was just as well. She wasn't sure dating one of Torre's teachers was the smartest thing to do, and while Max was a nice guy, maybe—well, just maybe he was too nice. Had her attraction to bad boys really burned out after Sal? Sometimes she wasn't so certain.

Hal and Lydia were yammering happily about menu selections—"You don't have anything against veal, do you?" Lydia asked—when Josie realized she needed some air. She excused herself and found her way out to the country club's terrace. It would be chilly out there, but she looked forward to the bracing air to straighten out her head.

What she did not expect was company, but she found some anyway. As she teetered onto the stone patio, she caught sight of two dark figures huddled together. Something told Josie it would be a good idea not to get any closer, but when her heel caught between the edges of two paving stones she lost her balance, and a small, involuntary yelp escaped her lips. From her supine position she saw who the figures were. One was Billy, who was leaning with his back against the terrace's wrought iron railing; the other, facing toward him and gazing up with her hands on his shoulders was Marisa Markle.

For a long moment, everyone stood frozen as if in a staged tableau. Frantically, Josie wondered how she was going to extricate herself from this situation with her own or anyone's dignity intact, but she needn't have worried.

At that moment, Dr. Nobler swung open the door to the terrace and shouted, "Mr. Stand? Billy? Are you out here? Ah, thank goodness. Mr. Stand, we just got a call. I'm sorry, it's about your wife. An ambulance has been called to your house. I'm afraid MaryAnn was found unconscious."

CHAPTER 8:

New Year's Eve

The story, by the time it made the rounds and landed at the Thorns' New Year's Eve party, went like this: MaryAnn Stand hadn't attended the Casino Night party because she had a (quote unquote) headache. After she put the kids to bed and the new housekeeper had gone home for the night, she (quote unquote) lost her balance, and tumbled down a flight of stairs. It was an amazing coincidence that young Mindy, whose mother was at the fundraiser and whose young brother was sleeping over at a friend's, had tired of being home alone and taken a stroll around the neighborhood. Good thing the Stands' garage door was accidentally left open when Mindy heard a cry and a thud. The girl had the terrific presence of mind to enter the Stands' house and, finding MaryAnn unconscious, dial 911 and then call Celeste on her cell phone.

Josie, serving her New Year's *vitello tonnato* entrée, had heard it all before. Tonight, though, the tale was recounted by the Thorns and by the Luffhausers for the benefit of Dan and Diane Fitzpatrick. As the only New Year's dinner party guests whose children attended Our Lady of Perpetual Sorrows, the Fitzpatricks were understandably a little bit out of the loop.

Like most people hearing the tale for the first time, Dan and Diane were simultaneously impressed with and aghast at young Mindy's bravado. Why, there could have been an intruder in the house making that noise, and goodness knows what possessed a thirteen-year-old girl to wander around her neighborhood alone at that hour. They hoped her mother had given her a good talking to.

Still, it had all worked out for the best for poor Mrs. Stand, everyone agreed. MaryAnn was not badly hurt, thank goodness, and was now (quote unquote) away for a while, getting some rest.

Not for the first time, Josie wondered if there was more to the story. When she'd asked her son if he knew what his classmate could possibly have been thinking, Torre had simply shrugged, but she could have sworn she saw his right eye twitch just the tiniest bit. It was an affectation she recalled in his father, when answering a question like "Sal, didn't we have a lot more cash than this in our checking account?" with an answer like, "Gee, I didn't notice (twitch). Who knows where the money goes, huh babe?"

But Mindy's motives were the least of Josie's concerns about that night. She hoped that in all the excitement that followed her own inopportune appearance on the country club patio, Billy had forgotten that she had witnessed his *tête-à-tête* with Marisa. But somehow she didn't think so.

Billy had been calling Josie for the past week, but she'd punched "Ignore" into her cell phone whenever his number came up. He'd even brought the twins into Cooler at the Shore the day after Christmas, but she'd ducked into the back when she saw them parking outside, leaving Jorge to take their order. She didn't want to hear any explanations, apologies, or lies. She just wanted to forget the whole thing.

Fortunately, the dinner party conversation moved on to other topics. Lydia, whose ire about Persephone's admissions deferral had resurfaced after its brief hiatus, wanted to discuss the difference between the Country Day and OLPS curricula. Dan and Diane were only too happy to boast about the exorbitant amount of homework their children labored over each evening.

"Why the spelling words alone take them *hours*," Diane volunteered. "But, honestly, I expect to see one of them at the Scripps National Bee one of these days."

"Yeah," Dan chimed in. "Enough with those Indian kids winning all the spelling titles. We need to get Americans back in the saddle. Win one for the Gipper."

Lydia would have turned pea green with envy had the shade not clashed with her tangerine hostess gown. Spelling! Persephone hadn't seen a spelling list since second grade, when Preston Nobler adopted Organic Language Arts. "Spelling is just a silly convention," he'd said. "Why should our learners waste time memorizing where i's and e's go when they could be *thinking* instead?"

"And Danny junior is doing long division already," Diane added. "You know, sometimes I think it's a bit much for second grade, but he does seem to rise to the occasion."

"It'll be well worth it, I'm sure," Dan chimed in. "There's nothing like a firm foundation in the fundamentals once you get to higher mathematics."

Lydia fumed. Maybe Persephone wouldn't have struggled with math all these years if that imbecile Nobler hadn't tossed out the Lower School's former program and brought in Everyman's Math with its "creative new algorithms." Everyman's Math didn't waste time on trivialities like solving long division problems to the second decimal point. As far as the masterminds behind it were concerned, the answer to a division problem was a whole number and an "R" for remainder, signifying only that there was "a little something left over." You'd hate to be the guy trying to land on Mars with that level of precision in your calculations.

Diane and Dan continued to wax eloquent about their children's academic feats, while Lydia wondered if it would be possible to successfully sue Country Day if Persey did not make the cut at Brown. Mentally, she prepared an opening statement: *Ladies and gentlemen of the jury, we will prove that Preston Nobler, through egregious idiocy, has deprived my daughter of her rightful legacy…*

Hal noticed his wife's attention wander and took the opportunity to steer the conversation in another direction.

"All this talk about math has me thinking about the economy," he said. "You know, we're seeing enough green shoots lately that I think the time is getting ripe for an IPO. Dan, have I told you about the opportunity to get in on the ground floor of Ergo-Geri?"

Dan took the bait eagerly. "Ergo-Geri? Is it a way to beat this god-awful up and down market? The damn S&P's one step forward, two steps back."

"Bah, the S&P's for suckers," Hal opined. "Of course, it's not every day a sure thing like this comes along."

Clearing dishes, Josie found herself lingering a bit longer than she had to. A sure thing? The words both intrigued and alarmed her. A sure thing was what Sal used to say, way too often, about a big bet that would help him to break even at last. It was a sure thing that Green Bay would beat Dallas in the '98 Super Bowl (they lost by a touchdown); or that the Braves would trounce the Yankees in the '99 World Series (they were creamed in four games); or that the three-year-old filly To the Moon Alice would take the third race at the Monmouth track (the poor horse got spooked by a flashbulb and pitched her jockey clear into the bleachers).

But this was different, wasn't it?

Josie took in her surroundings. The Thorns' well-appointed dining room, with its Chippendale cherry wood table and chairs, and its sideboard teeming with Baccarat, must mean Hal knew something about making real money—and Hal was right about the market. No matter what else was going on in her life, Josie had been sure to squirrel away a little money each month for Torre's college fund since the day he was born. It was money she'd kept hidden from Sal; she'd set it aside time and time again, even when it meant depriving herself of something she sorely needed, or repeatedly mending Torre's clothes rather than buying him new ones. But the money hadn't grown the way everyone said it would. One event after another—the dot com bust, terrorism scares, the Great Recession, a U.S. credit downgrade, insolvent Europeans, and God only knew what was next—had conspired to keep her conservative allotment of index funds right where they were a decade before.

Despite her best efforts, Torre now had exactly $21,406 to his name. The sum wouldn't cover a single semester at the kind of top school she was confident her boy could get into. Last time she checked the College Board website, MIT was running over $50,000 a year for tuition, room and board, a sum she knew would go up relentlessly over the next several years no matter the economy. What if Hal was really on to something? Could it really be that easy? Josie hoped Ergo-Geri would still be up for discussion in a few minutes—and knowing Hal she bet it would—but for now, she could think of no good reason to prolong her presence in the dining room. It was clearly time for dessert.

Juggling a stack of silverware and dishes, she teetered into the Thorns' recently renovated state of the art kitchen. It was the sort of kitchen—Viking range, twin ovens, sub-zero freezer, granite countertops—that clearly conveyed the message, "No one who lives here actually cooks."

"Hey, let me help you with those," someone said. Peering out from behind her platters, Josie saw Persephone heading toward her with open arms.

"Oh, it's okay, Persey, I can manage."

But Persey extricated the top few plates from Josie's stack and placed them in the industrial-sized stainless steel sink. "Don't be silly, Mrs. Messina. I can't believe you're doing this all by yourself."

Josie could barely believe it either, but it was New Year's Eve after all, and she could not bring herself to enlist Pete or Jorge, both of whom had infinitely more exciting things to do. Even Torre had offered to lend a hand, but she had shipped him off for an overnight at his friend Josh's house, assuring him that cooking, serving, and cleaning up after a gourmet dinner for six was no big deal for her to handle solo.

"What are you doing here, Persey? It's New Year's!"

Persephone looked crestfallen, and Josie was sorry she'd stated the obvious. Had a date stood her up? Had she been left out of some social event? It was hard to imagine. She knew from Torre that Persey was the quintessential popular girl, and she certainly looked the part—although thinner than usual, Josie noted. But the shadow that had clouded Persey's expression lasted only a moment, and Josie thought perhaps she had only imagined it as the girl assured her that she would, of course, be going out later.

"Hey, my friends and I won't even get started until you guys are winding down, Mrs. Messina. Really, let me give you a hand. I'm just hanging around."

"Well, sure, but why don't you let me fix you a plate first?" Josie offered. "You must be hungry by now."

"Well...that's veal, isn't it?" She wrinkled her nose at the remnants in the sauté pan.

"Uh, yeah, it is. *Tonnato*, in tuna sauce."

"I'm sorry, Mrs. Messina, I don't eat veal. Those cute little calves, those cramped little crates, you know."

Josie sighed. She did know. An omnivore by nature and upbringing, she too drew the line at veal, personally, but when customers requested it—well, business was business.

"Understood," she said. "How about an appetizer? There are still plenty of meatball skewers."

"No beef," said Persey. "Too many growth hormones."

"Okay, then some Caprese salad."

"Tomatoes are nightshades."

"No good, right?"

Persey nodded solemnly.

"I know, some dessert. I'm serving zabaglione with strawberries."

"Allergic to strawberries."

Wow, Josie thought, no wonder the poor girl looked like a stiff breeze would flatten her.

"But, hey, let me help you make the dessert at least. I love to cook," she said.

"You do?" Josie said. *You just don't like to eat*, she thought.

"Yup. When I was growing up, I cooked all the time. Carmen taught me."

"Who's Carmen?"

"The cook." Persey laughed, as though this should have been obvious.

Of course, Josie thought. *In this world, kids cooked with the cook. Did they garden with the gardener?* she wondered.

"We had the best times. We made all kinds of things—desserts especially, like flan. Is zabaglione like flan?"

"I guess you could say that. It's flan-ish."

"Every culture has its version of custard," Persey mused. "It's a universal comfort food. Zabaglione, flan, crème brulée."

"Why, I guess you're right," Josie agreed. For someone who had so many reasons not to eat, Persey certainly knew a lot about gastronomy.

As it turned out, Persey seemed like a natural when it came to cooking. Josie watched, duly impressed, as her self-appointed sous chef deftly separated eggs with the flick of a wrist and carefully, almost lovingly, whisked into the yolks the sugar that Josie handed her.

"Now we add the grated lemon peel," Josie said, "and a drop of cinnamon and vanilla extract. And now...shit. Oh, excuse me. Crap. Er, sorry. Damn!"

"What's the matter, Mrs. Messina?"

"I forgot the marsala wine."

"That's kind of critical, right?"

"Right." She slumped onto a kitchen stool.

"Wait! What about something here?" Persey reached up and opened a cupboard, revealing a cluster of liqueur bottles perched on a lazy Susan.

Josie jumped up and happily spun the bottles around until she spied just the thing. Grinning, she plucked a bottle of Grand Marnier from the turntable with her right hand and gave Persephone a high five with her left.

Josie poured a bit of the Grand Marnier into the egg mixture, and then placed the bowl over a saucepan of barely simmering water. She showed Persey how to beat the custard until it thickened. "Do it until the volume triples," Josie instructed, and Persephone did so, precisely. This was the kind of math with which she felt utterly comfortable.

The duo was pouring the zabaglione into strawberry-filled serving dishes when Hal swung open the kitchen door.

"Well, hello, honey pie." He grinned at his daughter. "I didn't think you were in here. Mom just sent me in to see how Josie was doing with the dessert."

Translation: What's taking her so long? Josie thought.

"We're doing just great, thanks," she said. "It turns out Persey is quite the assistant."

"Really?" Hal beamed at his child. "You know, I remember when you used to spend a lot of time in the kitchen, pumpkin. You and...and...what was her name?"

"Carmen," she offered.

"Yeah, her," he agreed. "She made a mean, um, what do you call it?"

"Flan," she said.

"Yeah, flan! Right."

"Well, let me just bring these in," Josie said as she placed six dessert dishes on a tray.

"Oh, let me carry those," Hal offered.

"No, no, I'm fine."

"No, I insist."

"Hey, I'll bring them in," Persey interrupted. "It'll give me a chance to show off my handiwork." She swept the tray into her arms and exited to the dining room before anyone could protest.

Hal smiled at Josie. "Wow, she's really into it, isn't she? I haven't seen her this excited about anything in a while. Stressful times, you know—college admissions and all that." Hal turned back toward the dining room but changed his mind. "Say, while I'm in here, I think I'll grab a bottle of Armagnac. Now where are those—?"

"The liqueurs?" Josie asked, opening the cupboard from which the Grand Marnier had come. "Right here."

"Why, so they are," he said. "*Hmmm*, Armagnac or something else?" he muttered, slowly spinning the turntable as he hunted for his prize.

Josie watched for what seemed like a long moment as Hal considered his options from among the expensive bottles. His comment about college had her thinking once again about just how much money some people had—and some people didn't. She hesitated for the briefest moment, then decided to broach Hal's favorite topic.

"Mr. Thorn—"

"Hal, please, *Hal*."

"*Hal.* I was wondering. You know, I was thinking about your company? You know, the nursing home chair company?"

"Ergo-Geri."

"Yes, Ergo-Geri. Um, you've mentioned you're taking on investors?"

"Yup," said Hal, moving his eyes between a bottle of Chambord and one of Lillehammer. "Say," he said, holding up the Lillehammer, "do you like the taste of lingonberries?"

"Lingonberries? Can't say I've tried them?" said Josie. Damn, she was ending every sentence like a question again. She'd thought she was getting over that. She had to calm down and ask for what she wanted. No beating around the bush.

"Um, I was wondering? That is, I think I might like to invest some money. You know, if I could. My son's college fund? I mean, it's not much, but I really need to do something with it? Seeing Persey makes me realize how fast this is all going to go."

Hal put the liqueurs down on the counter and turned to face Josie with what she would later remember as a kind of funny look. She couldn't tell if he was pleased that she'd asked, or appalled. Maybe it was a faux pas, asking him about investing like this, but she simply didn't know the etiquette of such things.

"College fund?" he asked. "Just how much money are we talking about here?"

"Well, around twenty thousand?"

His forehead tensed. As Josie would later recall, he appeared to have trouble meeting her eyes. "College is important, Josie. Don't get me wrong, Ergo-Geri is a sound investment, but still… there's always some risk."

"Well, if the past few years are any indication, I gather everything has some risk."

"Yes, of course, of course," he agreed. "Certainly. Well"—he coughed and put the Lillehammer back in the cupboard—"let me think about it. I'll get back to you, all right?" He tipped the flask of Chambord in her direction. "And happy New Year," he said as propelled himself quickly through the door to his waiting guests.

Later that night, as Hal peered out of his bedroom window and watched Josie drive away, he made his first and only New

Year's resolution. It had nothing to do with his plan, for that would remain in place. It was a flawless plan that had evolved almost a year ago, when Ergo-Geri's rehabilitative loungers started malfunctioning and ejecting senior citizens from their seats like cannon fodder. When his engineers had been unable to find a financially viable fix, he'd let the research and development staff go, preparing to close up shop. But then it dawned on him, as it had on so many other durable medical equipment vendors whose market was the elderly, that all one really needed to make a killing in the DME business were blank doctor's prescription pads and lists of Medicare patient numbers. It was as easy to purchase both of these on Florida's black market as it was to buy fries at McDonald's.

Of course, the scam couldn't go on forever. Every few years, some ball busters at *Sixty Minutes* would run an exposé on Medicare fraud and shame the Feds into cracking down for a while. Most of the hucksters would crawl into the woodwork for a bit, then reinvent their companies and start over—but not Hal. He was tired of the rat race. That was why he'd come up with his brilliant idea: Soak a bunch of filthy rich Little Fawners for "IPO" money, then head south of the border, where his lovely Carmen, first lady of flan, awaited.

But take college money from the mom of that nice boy who helped Persey with her math? Nope. No way. Hal would find a reason to turn Josie down. After all, he had his values.

• • •

Language Arts Journal, January 2 Mindy Battin

Everyone is asking me what it feels like to be a hero. <u>It feels pretty good</u>. Especially since everybody believed me about what happened. Even my Mom.

Of course the one person I hoped would be really impressed hasn't even bothered to talk to me.

It's okay. I'll come up with something.

I know I will. <u>I feel sure.</u>

CHAPTER 9:

Diversity Day

January 3
FROM: Dr. Preston Nobler
TO: All Faculty and Administrative Staff
RE: LFCD Diversity Day

Happy New Year all, and welcome back. This is going to be a very exciting year. Of course, our very successful Givers of Knowledge Capital Campaign continues full speed ahead. (Stay tuned for details on a special upcoming Valentine's Day fundraising event.) In addition, I have decided to inaugurate a new tradition here at LFCD: Diversity Day!

Diversity Day will take place a week from Monday on Martin Luther King, Jr. Day. Fortunately, LFCD has never before observed MLK Day, while most other New Jersey schools schedule it as a holiday. This works in our favor, since on that day we plan to invite to our school minority schoolchildren from surrounding areas, so that they may get to know us and we may get to know them.

Country Day Rainbow Recruiters (CDRRs), kindly meet with me in the auditorium at 3 p.m. today. We will begin planning our very special program for LFCD's First Annual Diversity Day.

Benjamin Jakes hunched closer to his computer monitor and pushed the bridge of his heavy glasses toward his nose. He scrutinized his poker hand once more. He had a pair of sixes in the hole. Better than nothing, but still, the hands of two of his online opponents looked like they might have potential.

"What do you think?" he asked the young boy peering over his shoulder.

"Go all in," said Torre. "Now."

"I don't know," Jakes hesitated. Was the kid right? He ran the probabilities that every serious Texas Hold'em player knew: Four to one odds you'll win with a pair in the hole against a lower pair; just a one in fifteen chance a player will hit a flush when he's dealt two cards of the same suit. That meant—

"Do it," urged Torre. "I've got a feeling."

Jakes took a deep breath and plunked all his virtual chips down. Several players saw his bet; a few folded. In the end, the jackpot was his.

"Well, what do you know?" breathed Jakes, turning to high five his star pupil, now turned mentor. A few more months of this and he could bow out of this penny ante teaching racket for good. Too bad he couldn't take Torre with him to Vegas for one of those master level tournaments. He'd love to find a way to make even more money from this poker racket.

"Hey Mr. Jakes," said Torre, glancing at the clock on the classroom wall, "I'm sorry but I've got to go to the assembly. It's almost time for me to give my speech."

The boy shuddered visibly. He'd been pressed into service by Dr. Nobler to "say a few words" to the potential scholarship students and parents invited to LFCD for Diversity Day. The thought of public speaking made his stomach churn, but the headmaster had insisted that he was the perfect example of how scholastic skills paved the road to success.

"Don't worry, young man," Dr. Nobler had insisted. "Why, I'll write the talk myself and all you'll have to do is read the words. Public speaking's no big deal at all. In fact, it's a breeze. You know the best advice ever given on the subject? Just imagine that everyone watching you is in their underwear."

Torre had turned crimson right there in the headmaster's office, suddenly having no choice but to visualize hundreds of people gawking at him—some of them his own teachers and classmates, including the admirably developing Mindy—clad in bras and boxers and what all. Who in God's name thought that was good advice? Still, in the end he'd agreed to speak. What choice did he have, really? He was keenly aware that a full scholarship student didn't have much in the way of bargaining power.

With a sigh, Benjamin Jakes logged off www.straightflush.com and clapped Torre across the back as he walked him to the door. "I feel for you, buddy," he said.

His sentiment was sincere. He didn't relish the thought of speaking before a crowd either, and was noticeably more at ease working with students one-on-one than he was explaining programming principles to a roomful of staring kids. Of course, he was happiest when working with Torre, especially now that he had discovered Torre's uncanny ability to help him accrue an exponentially growing nest egg. Best of all, growing rich through online gambling was—despite some brewing controversy—still just this side of legal, and if his helper was underage, well, that was no problem. After all, he never let Torre place any bets himself, or even so much as click on a card. The brilliant boy was just the angel on Jakes's shoulder, steering him toward a heaven that would be far, far away from Little Fawn Country Day.

Of course, Jakes had dues to pay before he went anywhere. He'd made a promise to Nobler; after all, the headmaster was the only one who would give him a job after his industrial espionage trial, even though he was cleared of all charges. (The stupid Feds couldn't pin anything on him because they couldn't figure out his algorithms. If they could have figured them out, they'd be working for Google, not the government.) Nobler, who had followed the trial in the papers with great interest, sought Jakes out when he was stone-broke from paying all those damned lawyers and made the erstwhile defendant an offer he couldn't refuse. But once Jakes discharged his obligation, that pompous little butterball could eat his dust.

Speaking of his obligation, Jakes was feeling lucky. He parked himself at his computer screen once more, cracking his knuckles and wriggling his fingers in the air before allowing them to alight on the keyboard. The last time he had tried this he was so close—so close. Maybe today was the day. He logged onto http://www.state.nj.us/education, and then drilled down to the site's employee portal.

Administrative Privileges Required, the screen said.

"Yeah, right," Jakes snorted. A chimpanzee could get through this firewall.

Enter user name and password.

Hmmm. Whom should he be today? Jakes entered a few rudimentary commands, scanned a list of system users, and selected a Ms. Ida Baumberg, Assistant to the Commissioner, as his proxy. A few more keystrokes and he was assigning the hapless Ms. Baumberg a new password. "Let's see," he murmured. Then, thinking about Nobler again, typed in *windbag1*.

Jakes checked Ms. Baumberg's e-mails and found exactly what he'd been hoping for. At last, versions of the coming NJ ASS exams had been posted for the commissioner's final review. He had only to tap into the mainframe to view them. Months of trolling the Department of Education's network had readied him for just such a challenge. He tapped happily on his keyboard:

```
HttpSniffer::const=pcktHdr*hdr  u_char=short  htype(ntoh
s)>Ethernet>type;break;default;return=NULL()    handle=o
penstream&&lookupDevice(iterator=Error  buffer)  intPay-
load; return delete; tcpSize http Packet <<Next() parse fprint
ipLenth complete<>
```

The high tech hieroglyphics quickly got him into the mainframe. He was happy as a preteen in a video arcade. For the next step, he needed a Trojan horse. He accessed a legitimate tool that security administrators used to locate holes in their systems, and that others with less noble intentions used to take advantage of those very same vulnerabilities. Within minutes, he'd found an open gate. Talk about a jackpot! Here was every grade level's version of the standardized tests that would be administered to every private school in the state in six weeks' time.

Jakes couldn't wait to tell Nobler "mission accomplished." He decided he'd stick around and wait until after the Diversity Day assembly so he could share the good news as soon as possible. He downloaded his booty onto a flash drive and then covered his tracks by reinstating Ida Baumberg's former password. He strolled over to his classroom window, opened it, and pulled a pack of Camels from his pocket. He lit one and took a drag, exhaling the smoke out into the frigid January air.

He was especially pleased with himself, not only because he'd so facilely breached the NJ DOE's network, but also because he had done so without the assistance of his star pupil. Truth be told, regardless of Nobler's elaborate plan, Jakes had recently grown uncomfortable with the idea of involving the boy in an illicit activity. In spite of himself, even in spite of the envy he nursed toward Torre's incomparable skills and instincts when it came to computer code, he had grown to like the kid. He preferred not to play a part in possibly sabotaging a life that clearly had such upside potential.

• • •

Sitting backstage in the Little Fawn Country Day auditorium, Moses scrunched all his six feet and four inches into a middle school-sized desk chair and wondered, once again, how the hell he had gotten into this. One minute he and his wife had been enjoying themselves at the elegant New Jersey Performing Arts Center, Newark's crown jewel, sampling the buffet dinner that followed Moses's induction ceremony into the New Jersey Hall of Fame. The room had been filled with dignitaries, from Newark's media darling mayor to the state's famously penny-pinching governor (who, despite his reputation, had apparently spared no expense for this star-studded gala), and with fellow honorees that included Danny DeVito, Jack Nicholson, Susan Sarandon, writer Judy Blume, and astronaut Wally Schirra. Moses and Delia had been mingling happily, thrilled to be in such distinguished company, but the next minute, Moses had felt a tap on his shoulder and looked down to discover none other than Dr. Preston Nobler.

"Mother and I buy tickets every year," he had promptly explained, beaming across the room at the diminutive octogenarian, who had somehow managed to corner Frankie Valli at the buffet's carving station. "Ah, I see Mom found her favorite celebrity!"

Although Delia managed to politely excuse herself to chat with Fran Lebowitz, Moses had found himself trapped in a conversation with Dr. Nobler that he could only manage to end by agreeing—far too hastily, he thought in retrospect—to speak at the following Monday's Diversity Day assembly at Little Fawn Country Day. Trying to explain to Delia after the party why she might want to head home on her own, Moses rationalized that extending his stay would give him a chance to see Billy on Sunday. Billy had put in the briefest of appearances at the Hall of Fame event, but bowed out after officially inducting his old bandmate and singing one song. He'd chosen "Pick Six," his famous ode to a Bayonne trash collector who was crushed by a trash masher after losing his winning lottery ticket in a landfill. Billy explained to the Joneses that he needed to get home and spend some time with the twins, who were so upset by their mom's long absence.

Moses was able to spend part of the next day with Billy. His old pal had been glum and preoccupied with trying, unsuccessfully, to reach someone on his cell phone. Nevertheless, he did manage to get something out of him.

"She was *drinking*," Billy said of MaryAnn. "Drinking in secret. I mean, it was crazy. You remember she never used to drink at all. I knew something was up. She kept, you know, just disappearing, but I told myself it wasn't happening. I'm an asshole."

"Hey, come on, man. It won't help her for you to get down on yourself. She needs your help with her problem," Moses had counseled.

"I'm the problem," he insisted. "She never liked the limelight. It's been getting worse and worse. She should be married to a regular person—a dentist, an accountant. Have a normal life."

"Yeah, man." Moses tried to lighten the mood. "Well, maybe you're right. I'll introduce her to my tax attorney as soon as she's better."

But Billy hadn't cracked a smile or offered a return jab of sarcasm. Instead he'd sighed mournfully and shook his head. "Whatever. She deserves better than me."

Whatever? Moses couldn't believe what he was hearing. Was Billy actually ready to give up on his marriage? Why? He thought back to what MaryAnn had told him months before, and decided to put it on the table.

"Billy, listen—awhile back, before Thanksgiving, MaryAnn talked to me. She told me—this sounds crazy, man, I know, but she said she thought there was another woman in your life."

In his heart of hearts, Moses was expecting, or at the very least hoping, for a flat out denial. Instead his friend blanched and looked down at his boots. Moses just stared at him and then, suddenly, the opportunity to pursue this potential moment of truth evaporated as little Lucy's voice rang out from the kids' upstairs playroom.

"Daddy, Daddy, come here. My Barbie lost her shoe."

"'Scuse me," Billy had muttered, with an evident note of relief.

It was then that Moses, admittedly, crossed a little bit of a line. Noticing that Billy had left his cell phone on the kitchen counter, he picked it up, clicked on Recent Calls, and then clicked again on Calls Dialed. The listing said, "Josie. Josie. Josie."

• • •

Backstage at Little Fawn Country Day's Diversity Day assembly, Moses was so distracted by his unsettling reverie that he barely registered the fact that someone had plunked down beside him.

"Hey, hello, Mr. Jones," said the boy. "Wow. What are you doing here?"

Moses recognized the boy from Thanksgiving at the Wild Bay Food Bank.

"Hey, dude, I remember you, but I'm sorry I don't exactly remember your name."

"Torre. Torre Messina. I was at Thanksgiv—"

"Hey, yeah. Torre. I remember you, and your mom. Well, what are you doing here? Shouldn't you be out there?" He nodded in the direction of the auditorium's seats, which were filling with LFCD students and Diversity Day visitors.

"I wish," admitted Torre. "Dr Nobler's making me give a speech." The boy sighed and slumped his shoulders as he looked down at his notes.

Moses chuckled and clapped him on the back. "Me too, dude. I feel your pain." He smiled. "Watcha gonna talk about?"

Torre handed Moses the five-by-eight inch index card he'd been studying.

I'm happy to be here with you today as a living testament to the magnanimous scholarship outreach program of Little Fawn Country Day. Here at Country Day, I have been introduced to the highest academic standards and upstanding traditions…

"You write this?" Moses asked.

"Nah."

"Nobler?"

"Yup."

Moses remembered what middle school was like. As a big, athletic kid, he wasn't picked on much, but poor Torre didn't look like the kind of kid who could pull off a speech like this without getting hammered by his classmates afterward.

"You like it at this school?" he asked.

"Um, yeah. Yeah, pretty much," Torre answered. He had to admit it wasn't nearly as boring as his last school, though he still missed his old buddies.

"Well, dude, why don't you just say what's in your heart?"

Torre stared up at him. "Uh…because Nobler would have a cow?"

Moses laughed aloud. He really felt for this kid. That crazy headmaster putting all those pretentious words in his mouth, and his mom—well, God knew what was going on there.

"Okay," he said, "I hear you, man. But you know, sometimes it's cool to improvise."

Torre was tempted to ask for some ideas, but just then Mrs. Chapel bustled in, looked at her watch, and signaled to Moses. "Mr. Jones, you're up next," she said briskly.

"Wish me luck," he said, offering the boy a high five, and walked out onto the stage.

"*Bene rem gere*," Mrs. Chapel called after him. "Do a bang-up job."

By this point in his life, Moses had lots of experience talking to kids in settings like this. He knew people considered him a good role model and an inspirational figure, especially here in his home state, but what he thought made him such a good speaker was that he never prepared a formal talk. He spoke extemporaneously, but he always communicated the same underlying message. Today was no different.

"Hey, everyone," he began after the rousing applause that greeted him subsided. "I didn't exactly plan on being here today, but your headmaster asked me to say a few words. Now, I know you probably want to hear about my football career"—he broke off to allow a fresh round of applause—"or maybe my music." The kids clapped some more. "But the topic today is education." Some in his audience laughed; others groaned.

"Hey, it's not so bad! Because you know what? It all adds up to the same thing—the power inside you. People always ask me how I got so good at certain things, and I'm here to tell you how. Did the good Lord give me some natural abilities? Yes, He did, just the same as He gave you. I don't know what He gave each of you, but trust me, He gave you a gift. But that's not enough. You've got to figure out what that gift is, and then—this is even harder—you've got to make up your mind to unwrap that gift and figure out what to do with it.

"I've been successful doing what I find fun. I think music is fun. I think football is fun. And you know what? I even thought schoolwork was fun." More groans punctuated his remark. "Yeah, it's true, but here's the thing: Nothing's really that much fun until you're kind of good at it. And how do you get good at anything? Drive. Focus. Practice, and then more practice. And then even more.

"I know a lot of you are here today because you've been told this fine school is opening up room for some more scholarship students. Well, some of you are going to get those scholarships, and some of you are not. That's just the way it goes. Maybe this particular blessing isn't in the cards for you—at least not right now. But you know what? It won't make one bit of difference. That's right. Not one bit. *If*'—he paused and swept his gaze across the room—"*if* you tap into that drive, that focus, that power in you.

"This is a nice place, a fancy building, and the headmaster tells me it's about to get even fancier. But you don't *need* a fancy school. You don't *need* a great big building. If you don't come here, fine. Go back to your school and make it a better place. Stop wasting time. Yeah, I know you're good at that, but stop it. Tell your teachers you want more work to do. Yes, *more.* Tell them Moses said so. Tell your parents to get involved in that school. Tell them to go over your homework with you and make sure you get any extra help you need when you need it. And tell them to take you to the library, and that you want to read with them every night before you go to bed. And if they tell you they don't have time, you tell them to make time. Tell them Moses said so. And if you think you're too old to snuggle up and read with your parents, well then you read on your own. Who says so?"

"Moses!" the kids cheered.

"You have lots of questions about the world. I know you do. A lot of the answers are in the books you'll read. And the questions that haven't been answered yet—well, guess what? You guys could be the ones to answer them, but only if you make up your mind to learn what's already out there. You can't reinvent the wheel until you know why it's round.

"I know it's cool to tell kids today, 'You can do anything you want to do.' Well, that's only part of the story. You can do anything you want *if* you make up your mind to put in the time. That's right, make up your mind to put in the time. Let that be your motto. Don't let anyone stop you. Don't let anyone tell you it's not possible, because it is possible. And don't let anyone tell you it's not up to you, because it *is* up to you.

"So let me hear you say your new motto. What are you gonna do at this school or any other? You're gonna…"

"Make up my mind to put in the time," came the audience refrain.

"And who says so?"

"Moses!"

Moses exited the stage to thunderous applause, and gave Torre a thumbs-up as Mrs. Chapel waved the boy onto the stage. For a moment Torre stared at him blankly, and it dawned on him that Torre could freeze. He wasn't used to having a twelve-year-old speak after he did, and he hadn't thought about it beforehand. Realizing he might be a tough act to follow, Moses made a spur of the moment decision. He turned, clapped a massive arm across Torre's shoulder, and walked with the boy back onto the stage.

Watching from the wings, the headmaster was agog. What the hell was Moses doing? He wasn't entirely pleased with Moses's speech, which he thought smacked of, well, anarchy. Now this? This wasn't part of the plan at all. Nobler had planned to introduce Torre himself, to show him off as a fine example of Country Day's benevolence.

But Moses and Torre were received by another hearty round of applause. There was nothing he could do to stop the momentum.

"Hey," Moses addressed his fans again, "I almost forgot. I want you to listen to a few words from my friend Torre here. Torre's a bright young guy who's going to speak to you from the heart. Right, my man?"

Torre blinked at the expectant audience as Moses stepped back into the shadows. He clasped his index card tightly, but he didn't look at it.

"Hey guys." He smiled, settling his gaze on the group of visiting students sitting in the first few rows. "Um, my name's Torre Messina, and I want to thank you all for coming today to our school's first annual Diversity Day."

So far, so good, Nobler thought.

"Our headmaster, Dr. Nobler, asked me to say a few words about what it's like to be a scholarship student here."

Okay, still good. The headmaster began to relax.

"Well, it's pretty cool," said Torre.

Not in the script, but still okay.

"Everyone's been really nice to me—the students and the teachers, too. There's a lot of opportunity here to learn stuff you might not get in a lot of other places."

Okay, so the kid was going to improvise, but he was still on message.

"But I have to say I agree with Mr. Jones."

Huh?

"I got to come here for free because I was pretty good at something, which for me happens to be math."

At the mention of the "m" word—not everyone's favorite subject—Torre could see some of the kids in the audience start to look dejected.

"But really I'm just lucky, I guess, because I found a thing I was good at pretty early. But I think everybody's probably really good at something, even if you don't know what it is yet. So, even if you don't get to come here, I think you should work hard at your schoolwork, and at everything you do, and figure out which thing you're best at and which makes you happiest.

"It's okay if you don't have the answers right now. My mom always said the best thing was to be curious and ask a lot of questions, and I think she's right. That's the best way to find out about stuff, and you can be curious anywhere. It doesn't matter if you're in Little Fawn or Lower Fawn or Wild Bay or anywhere."

What the hell is that little pipsqueak talking about?

"Well, so anyway—" Torre looked down and realized he'd never consulted his note card. Unsure of how to maneuver himself offstage, he flipped it over to his pre-scripted final sentence.

"Thank you again for joining us here today. It's our sincere pleasure to host all of you. And now, I'd like to introduce the Little Fawn Country Day Glee Club, featuring Mindy Battin, which will perform a medley of songs inspired by the late Dr. Martin Luther King."

As Mindy burst into the opening notes of a mash-up of "We Shall Overcome" and "The Wind Beneath My Wings", Nobler decided that under the circumstances, the wisest thing he could do was take a breather and calm down before he had to resume his master of ceremonies role. Letting himself out of the auditorium through a backstage exit, he stomped into the hallway, across the marble floor of the school's lobby, and into its ornate vestibule. His plan was to keep going in hopes that the frosty air outside would cool his temper, but he ran into Benjamin Jakes, who was sucking on yet another Camel.

"Dr. Nobler," Jakes greeted him. Somewhat embarrassed to be caught smoking on school grounds, the teacher instinctively moved the offending cigarette behind his back. "What are you doing out here? Assembly over already?"

The headmaster glared. "Over? No, it's not freaking over, but it's a goddamned disaster. People just saying whatever nonsense comes into their heads. They're—they're—insubordinate!"

"Who is?"

"That Moses Jones, for one, but I guess that's what you can expect from the likes of him," Nobler sputtered. "But then, to top it off—"

He felt a vein in his head throb. Talking about it was just making it worse, and he knew he had to collect himself before he went back onstage to wrap things up. The crowd would only put up with Mindy's warbling for so long.

"On top of that, *what?*" Jakes prompted.

"Never mind," he said. "And don't look at me like that. Give me one of those goddamned cigarettes."

Jakes fished out a Camel, handed it over, and offered a light. "Try to relax. I've got some good news for you."

Nobler inhaled a long drag and coughed. "You do?"

"Yeah. In fact, this is going to make your day."

"Okay, let's hear it."

"I got into the DOE system, and the test versions are ready. I can access the ASS."

"And?"

"And? Well, it's simple. I'll get you all the versions—grades two to twelve—every one. All you have to do is—"

"Is what, you numbskull?" Nobler snapped. "Do you expect me to just hand out copies of the test to our kids and ask them to memorize the answers? Don't you think that's a little, you know, *obvious*?"

"Well, no, but the teachers can use the tests to write lesson plans and—"

"Teach to the test! Never! Never! We're better than that here at Country Day. We're nurturing creativity, molding lifelong learners." He was horrified, as if someone had suggested his own mother didn't love him.

"Besides," he added, after a moment's thought, "it wouldn't work. We can't trust the teachers with this kind of sensitive information—at least, not all of them."

Jakes was crestfallen. He knew what was coming next.

"No," said Nobler. "I want you to stick with our original plan. I want you to find a way to get into the DOE Scantron system and alter the test results."

"The problem is that's way more complicated. I've been thinking about it. We can't just change the scores after the fact. That's too easy to catch. You know there's too much of a spotlight on test tampering these days. We have to get into the individual answer sheets, recode each one—"

"You and Boy Genius can pull it off. We discussed this. You just keep on bonding with him, then tell him you need his help with a security project you're working on for the state. The little thug will be thrilled to get a chance to do some hacking again, especially if it's for a 'good cause.' And Torre Messina can pull it off; I have faith. He's more than capable, I'm certain, even if you're not up to it."

Jakes stared down and ground out his cigarette with his shoe heel. God damn it, it was true. From what he'd seen, the kid was one of those naturals who could probably hack his way into the Department of Defense if he felt like it. Outfoxing the State Department of Education should be a cakewalk. The only problem was that he'd come to like the little son of a gun. What if something backfired?

"Jakes, look at me," Nobler insisted. "A deal's a deal. Am I right, or am I right?"

"It would appear you are correct," answered Jakes.

• • •

Josie beamed as the Diversity Day assembly disbanded. Along with the rest of the Country Day parents who had attended the festivities, she headed out to the parking lot as the students and teachers began touring the Rainbow Recruits around the LFCD grounds. She was proud of her son; despite his reluctance, he had given a heck of a speech, and she was more than a little thrilled that he had thought to mention her. *It was true*, she thought; she *had* always encouraged him to be curious. Maybe it was about time she claimed a little credit for herself.

As she made her way toward her van, other Country Day moms and dads gave her friendly waves, and several, including Brad and Emily, called out to her that Torre had done well. Somewhat incredibly, Josie actually felt as if she belonged. No one asked her to cater; she was just one of the gang. She felt buoyant, and basked in the gratitude she felt for everything that this school, for all its quirks, had done for her and her child.

It was always a good idea to relish such moments, for one never knew when they would come to an abrupt end. As Josie unlocked her vehicle, she felt a presence beside her, and looked up—way up—to greet the looming figure of Moses Jones. She tried to formulate a sentence, like "Hey, what a terrific talk you gave," or "Thanks for introducing Torre." But the grave look on his face stopped her from saying anything at all.

"You're Josie, right?" he asked.

"Why, yes. We met at the—"

"Yes, right, we did. Listen, Josie, let me ask you something."

"Er...okay? I mean...sure?"

"Don't you care about families?"

"Care about families? Do I care about families?" Josie drew a blank. Why would Moses Jones ask her such a bizarre question?

"Yes, like the Stands, for example."

Now she was more confused than ever.

"Because if you do, now's the time to put an end to it," he declared.

"*It?*" Josie racked her brain. He might as well have been speaking in Mandarin.

"You seem like a nice lady, Josie, and you have a great kid. Be happy with that and leave Billy alone."

With that, Moses turned and stomped off, his long gait carrying him across the parking lot in seconds. By the time Josie realized what he was getting at, he was gunning a shiny red Audi R8 onto the road.

That's when Josie slipped into the driver's seat of her van and started to laugh, and laugh—until she pounded on her steering wheel. Until tears streamed from her eyes.

CHAPTER 10:

Valentine's Dance

Students, Parents, Faculty
Come One, Come All To The

Love of Learning Valentine's Dance

at Little Fawn Country Day

Tickets: $200 per adult, $75 per student
(includes one free raffle ticket for a dream Hawaiian
vacation!)

All proceeds to benefit the
Givers of Knowledge Capital Campaign

Dress: Semi-formal

Persephone missed food. She missed the savory snap of a sea-salted potato chip; the cool, comforting gulp of a raspberry smoothie; and the sticky tingle of a hot buffalo wing. But most of all she missed chocolate: the flaked gooey crunch of a Twix cookie bar; the rich, bitter implosion of a dark Godiva truffle; the all-American melt-in-your-mouth goodness of a Hershey's Kiss. When she opened the box from Little Fawn Flora and discovered the single, elegant chocolate rose inside, she stroked it lovingly, and then sighed.

Persephone was still on a hunger strike, more or less, pending her admission to Brown University. In situations when she simply couldn't avoid eating lest she risk drawing attention to the bargain she'd made with the Universe, she nibbled daintily on the least caloric options she could find.

Later, looking back on it all, Persey would be grateful that she could never bring herself to stick her fingers down her throat. How anyone could force herself to throw up, she could never understand. Just remembering an epic bout of nausea she'd experienced on the Rolling Thunder ride at Six Flags Great Adventure when she was eleven made her shudder.

The first ten pounds Persey lost in the course of her current quest were greeted with congratulatory zeal at home and at school. Lydia shed not a tear at the departure of her daughter's baby fat, and Persey's fellow cheerleaders remarked, not without a twinge of envy, how awesome she looked in her uniform. The second ten pounds drew no alarm either, for everyone knew it was good to lose a little more weight than necessary so you'd have a little wiggle room to work with the next time you found yourself at a Super Bowl party or an all-you-can-eat sushi bar. But now that Persey was whittling away even more of her figure, some people were beginning to wonder if the girl had an "issue." And though she did not know it, one person in particular was determined to do something about the situation.

Hence the delectable rose, accompanied by a note reading: *Persey, Be my date for the Valentine's dance? Chip*

She couldn't help but giggle. Chip had always been kind of a cornball. No other boy she knew would come up with anything even remotely resembling this anachronistic romantic gesture. It reminded her of something out of one of those Cary Grant movies her mother liked to watch on AMC. But Chip was sweet and, she had to admit, awfully cute. She'd known him all her life, but lately they'd been shyly glancing at each other in a new way.

Persey closed the box, eschewing the chocolate rose, and texted Chip a romantic reply: *Thx 4 rose, k 2 dance. c u. xo P.*

• • •

When the hospitality committee sent out a request for parent chaperones for the "Love of Learning Dance," Josie was the first to volunteer. For one thing, she figured it would prevent anyone from hitting on her for catering. For another, it meant she could go "stag" and avoid tying herself to Max for the entire evening. Tonight, Josie was on a mission—two missions, actually. She absolutely had to speak with two men, and neither was the still smitten math teacher, much to his disappointment.

She hesitated only for a moment before snipping the tags off an above-the-knee cinnabar satin sheath she'd ordered online from Nordstrom's. With the cunning frugality that seemed to be unilaterally possessed by the ultra-wealthy, Emily had explained to her that returns for web orders went virtually unquestioned, regardless of whether or not a garment's tags were intact. So long as Josie didn't do anything drastic like spill a quart of paint on her frock, she could neatly refold it, slip it back into its plastic wrapping, and ship it back to the warehouse from whence it came. The $16.95 shipping and handling charge still made her wince a little, but things would be looking up if she could corner Hal tonight and get him to agree to take her investment in his company's public offering.

Surveying herself in the mirror, Josie hoped she resembled to at least some faint degree a woman of means—a woman who, in the eyes of Hal Thorn, could stand to lose twenty thousand dollars and laugh it off. Since her immersion in the Country Day milieu she had learned a few things: One was that, in this community at least, the appearance of success was at least as useful as actual success;

the other was that the rich knew all the angles. Take Emily—the ins and outs of retail returns were small potatoes compared to the other tricks she knew. Leave it to the Luffhausers to figure out a way to own a time-share on Kauai, donate one week's use to a non-profit raffle each year, and basically parlay that tax deduction into a free week for themselves. Priceless.

Josie let her mind wander for a moment, wondering what she would do if she actually won tonight's grand prize for that tropical vacation. A break from the kitchen would be nice, wouldn't it? Maybe she and Torre could load up on sunscreen and go during the Country Day spring break. Crystal blue waves, balmy beaches...yup, just her and her adolescent son. She shook her head and sighed.

And to think Moses Jones had actually mistaken her for a home wrecker. In a way, she supposed it was the greatest compliment she'd had in years.

•   •   •

Lydia, too, dreamed about the fair shores of the Aloha State as she fastened a baby pink cable wrap around her shoulders with a diamond pin. (Lilly Pulitzer's Valentine's collection having come through again with the perfect sartorial touch). She and Hal hadn't taken a vacation in over a year, and she had steadfastly refused to languish in some tacky Fort Lauderdale hotel while Hal did whatever he did to market those Ergo-Geri contraptions. It would be wonderful to have a real respite.

Perhaps a trip would even take her mind off some of the angst surrounding her daughter's college admissions decision. The suspense was becoming absolutely unbearable, and her patience with the Brown admissions staff—who, for reasons she could not fathom, would no longer speak with her when she called to extol another of Persey's virtues that perhaps had not been fully illuminated in her application—was wearing thin.

Thank goodness Persey seemed to be holding up better than she was. In fact, the girl had seemed quietly serene when she'd wafted in just moments ago to borrow a pair of hoop earrings.

That tie-dye tank dress with its little gathered waist was so flattering, too. It made her look delightfully tiny, almost elfin.

Lydia wondered if Persey was as taken with the Luffhauser boy as he obviously was with her. She suspected so. That would certainly explain her lack of appetite lately. There was nothing like first love to melt a few pounds away.

Lydia congratulated herself on how observant she was, and on how well she understood her adolescent child. That psych degree had not been for nothing!

• • •

Celeste also allowed herself to fantasize about a week in Kauai. The location would be the perfect meeting spot for her and Andy. She hadn't seen her husband in months—he was so busy with his global enterprises—but surely she could persuade him to hop a quick flight from the Far East for a romantic reunion. Couldn't she?

Of course that wouldn't give Mindy and Lars a chance to see their far-flung dad; maybe she could bring them along. But the kids were so wrapped up with their schoolwork and their friends, and Mindy was spending hours a day at her singing now, heartened by the fact that in two short years she could try out for *American Idol.* Well, on second thought, maybe they could just do some family Skyping—if she could figure out how that Skype thingie worked.

• • •

Hal busied himself with a second piece of pink-iced red velvet cake as he surveyed the Little Fawn Country Day gymnasium, which was decked out in full heart-shaped décor. God, he was tired of these blasted fundraisers, but he reminded himself that his command performances at such gatherings were numbered. Once he met up with Carmen in sunny Mexico, he would never again burden himself with a necktie or even a button-down shirt. Meanwhile, he knew events like this could only help Nobler's

Capital Campaign cash flow, and since that cash was flowing right into Hal's own Grand Cayman bank account, how could he really complain?

Besides, he could always find someone on whom to practice his charms at convivial events like this. Take that foxy kindergarten teacher—she looked positively R-rated in that short, one-shouldered number she was wearing. How come he never had a teacher like that? Forty years after kindergarten he still remembered Mrs. McGunfey, chin mole, jowls, and all. *Mrs. McDumpy.* Well, he guessed you couldn't expect to hold the attention of these video-dazed kids today with anything less than eye candy at the front of the class. He guessed—*shit!*

Hal saw Josie heading straight for him. Realizing there was no chance in hell of dodging her, he quickly composed his mouth into what he was quite sure was a debonair grin.

"Well, well, if it isn't Josie," he said, going straight for a compliment he hoped would deflect what he assumed was her preferred subject of investing in his company. "You've outdone yourself with this cake."

Josie laughed. "Fortunately, that's Luffhauser Farms' cake."

"Fortunately?"

"Yeah, I'm kind of, you know, going broke with all these fundraisers?"

"Ah, I hear you. We all know how that feels," he said. Crap, they were on the subject of money already. He assumed it wouldn't be long now.

"Hey, speaking of being broke, remember we were talking about my son's college fund?"

"Oh, yes. Yes, I remember. Well, the market's been edging up lately. Hopefully you've seen a little appreciation."

"A little, sure," she agreed, "but college is getting closer every day. From what I can see, the cost of tuition seems to keep go up no matter what else is going on in the economy."

Hal had to agree. Just thinking about the piles of money Persey's college fund had soaked up over the years made him wince. What the hell were these colleges doing with all that cold cash? For a moment he wondered if it would have been more lucrative to go into higher education than Medicare fraud.

"Hal, are you okay?"

"Oh, sorry, Josie; my mind wandered there. I was just thinking about, uh, how great the gym looks tonight."

"Ah, it sure does," she said, although she couldn't help but notice how rapidly an enormous ice sculpture of Cupid was melting onto the dessert table. "But as I was saying, well, do you remember you were going to think about letting me invest Torre's college money in your company's public offering?"

"Oh yes, sure. Your—what was it—twenty grand?"

"Around that."

"Well, Josie, here's the thing: unfortunately, we're just not able to accept investments in such, er, modest amounts."

"Oh? Well, it's not modest to me." *Damn*, she thought, *I shouldn't have admitted that.*

"Even so, we're really looking more at, um, institutional investors."

"Only institutional?" Josie recalled very well that Hal had offered his New Year's Eve dinner guests an opportunity to get in on the ground floor of Ergo-Geri.

"Well, and a few, er, close friends and family. That is, of course, if they're sufficiently liquid."

Josie eyed the melting ice sculpture again. *Maybe Cupid can invest*, she thought. *He's pretty liquid.* "Oh, I see."

Hal felt a genuine pang of guilt at her crestfallen expression. For a second, just the briefest moment, he considered the ramifications of agreeing to take her money. After all, twenty thousand was twenty thousand, and could go a long way south of the border. Besides, it certainly would cheer the woman up—in the short run. But, no; he had made himself a promise. He preferred to bilk the greedy and the gluttonous. He was, he reassured himself, the Robin Hood of white-collar crime.

"Really, Josie," he said, trying to let her down easy. "Someone in your situation is best off with a diversified portfolio of large value equities and mid-cap—"

"Got it," she said. She'd heard the same baloney from that dweeb at Fidelity who was looking after Torre's account, at least nominally. But she no longer believed the boilerplate investment patter. Since meeting her new best friends, she had witnessed the truth for herself: the rich got richer, and however they accomplished it, it certainly wasn't with a balanced portfolio of mutual funds.

Hal managed to look appropriately sheepish as he hastily excused himself. "Well, Josie, I don't want to monopolize you," he said, remembering that the best way to extricate oneself from an awkward conversation was to blame it on the other party (which was why he so frequently ended his phone conversations with "Hey, let me let you go.").

"Yes, I suppose I'd better do some actual chaperoning before this dance deteriorates into an orgy," she offered, freeing Hal to walk hastily across the room, straight in the direction of Marisa Markle, as it happened. He was so captivated by the sight of the alluring instructress, who seemed somewhat lonely as she licked the red and white icing off a heart-shaped cupcake, that he did not notice when he practically stepped on someone. It was Mrs. Chapel, who had been hovering nearby while he and Josie conversed.

Thanks to many long years of working for Preston Nobler, Mrs. Chapel was well accustomed to being treated as if she were invisible, and she deftly stepped out of his way. *How odd*, she thought as she mulled over the conversation she had just overheard. Hal wouldn't take Josie's investment, and her own broker had told her he'd found no Securities and Exchange public offering filings for a company called Ergo-Geri.

"*Suspicio*," she mumbled in Latin. "I smell a rat."

· · ·

Josie took a turn around the gymnasium, trying to simmer down. Of course she wasn't going to get in on any hot investment action. What made her think that was plausible? Look at these people. They weren't going to let the likes of her play in their sandbox, and that was that. Well, fine. She and Torre would figure something out; they always did. She wasn't going to compromise her dignity ever again by asking any of the Little Fawn crowd for favors. *The selfish bunch of—*

Realizing that this simmering down thing wasn't going as well as she'd hoped, Josie stepped through one of the gymnasium exit doors onto a staircase landing, then walked down a flight to another landing to clear her head from the din of music. But it seemed Persey Thorn and Chip Luffhauser had already claimed that patch of real estate for themselves. Josie blushed and mumbled an apology when she encountered the couple locked in what seemed to be a relatively chaste, but decidedly earnest, embrace. Maybe she should have broken up their tryst in her official role as chaperone, but who could be so heartless as to thwart young love on Valentine's Day of all days?

Turning on her heel, she walked two flights up, but that staircase landing had been staked out as well.

"Josie!" exclaimed Billy.

She froze, one foot hovering above the top stair. Then, instinctively, she pivoted. She'd wanted to talk to Billy tonight and clear the air, but she'd be damned if she was going to talk to him if he was waiting for a tryst with that...that *kinder tart.*

"Wait!" he called after her. "Where are you going? Josie, for God's sake, I've been trying and trying to reach you."

"Hey, I don't want to interrupt anything." Josie startled herself with the edge in her tone.

"Interrupt what?"

She just stared at him until she saw a light dawn behind his eyes.

"Oh, man. You mean...Listen, Josie, I'm just taking a breather. The twins are inside doing the chicken dance."

"Good," she said, making another move to leave. "Well, unlike you, I wouldn't want to miss that."

"Hey, wait. Stop. I know what you saw at the country club—or what you thought you saw. Listen, it was nothing. You got the wrong impression, I swear."

Josie flashed back in time to when she babysat young Billy. The grown man standing before her now had the same sheepish look he had both those times he'd crashed a baseball through her family's kitchen window. They were accidents, she knew, but how many times did you have to warn a kid about not playing ball in the driveway?

"Okay, look," he said. "It was just one of those moments, that's all. The kids' kindergarten teacher—she just got the wrong idea. Maybe I was flirting with her a little, you know? But nothing happened. It was just some crossed wires, I swear. I swear on my kids. I know I can be a jerk sometimes. I'm sorry."

"Billy, I'm not the one you need to apologize to."

"Listen, I know. It's complicated, though—that's the thing. That's one of the things I've been trying to tell you; MaryAnn's got some problems. She'd been drinking on the sly, but you know that's not like her."

"Maybe she got tired of your crossed wires."

"No, no, it started before that. That's the whole thing. It's been going on since before we moved back here. The shrinks in rehab say she has another problem she was trying to use the alcohol to help her with. She has agoraphobia. It's a fear—"

"I know what it is," said Josie.

He nodded. He had been surprised how much was known about agoraphobia. When he'd first heard the word, he'd thought MaryAnn had developed some irrational fear of rabbit's wool sweaters.

"That would be *angora*phobia," the psychologist had corrected him. "*Agora*phobia is an anxiety disorder, a fear of being in crowds or, in cases like your wife's, an escalating dread of simply being out in public. Sufferers fear they might panic and have no way to escape. We're not sure how or why it begins, but we do know that some people try to self-medicate with alcohol."

"MaryAnn's not an alcoholic, Josie," he went on. "For the record, I didn't drive her to drink by cheating on her, but I blame myself for being so out of touch. She loves me, I know that, but she was never comfortable being in the public eye. It's gotten worse and worse. I thought coming back home to Jersey would make it better, but Little Fawn isn't really home, is it?"

"I know what you mean," Josie agreed. "But Billy, what happens now?"

"She's getting therapy and she's in a support group. The doctors offered her Prozac, but she says she's not going from being dependent on one substance to being dependent on another. She's doing okay, but the shrinks want her to start getting out little by little."

"So, you're going to bring her home?"

"No, not yet. They want her to go out for little bits of time, like out to lunch or shopping or something. And the doctors say I shouldn't even be the one to take her at first, because, you know, the two of us can't go anywhere together without attracting attention. They asked if one of her girlfriends could take her. That's why I was trying to reach you."

"Me? I don't really know Maryann that well. By the time you guys were dating—"

"I know, I didn't see you so much then. You were always with Sal."

She sighed. "Don't remind me."

"But Josie, you're a Wild Bay girl. That's really home for MaryAnn. There's no one else she'd feel comfortable with around here. I mean, come on, who am I gonna ask?" He waved his hand limply in the general direction of the gymnasium, where the mothers of Country Day were no doubt comparing notes on who was wearing what, who was eating what, and who had bought how many raffle tickets. Josie had to admit Billy had a point.

"Okay, Billy, I'll do whatever I can. Of course I will."

"Thanks, Josie, thank you. We gotta stick together, right?"

"Okay, but listen Billy, there's something else we need to straighten out. You know your friend Moses?"'

"Yeah, what about him?"

"He gave me a lecture when I saw him on Diversity Day. He thinks we, er, he thinks you and I...you know?"

Billy looked at her blankly. Josie couldn't believe she actually had to say this aloud. "He thinks you and I were having...you know? An affair?"

They stared at each other in silence as similar memories unfolded in their minds: Josie watching Billy play stickball on their street; Billy skinning his knee and Josie applying a Band-Aid; the two of them hunched over Billy's English homework, as Josie tried to teach a decidedly uninterested Billy the difference between an adverb and an adjective.

Simultaneously, Josie and Billy channeled their mutual embarrassment into peals of laughter and then collapsed into each other's arms. If there was, during that embrace, even a fraction of a second where the thought of their relationship taking a carnal turn was as intriguing as it was disturbing, neither of them alluded to it, or would ever have admitted to it. In any case, they didn't really have the opportunity, for it was at that precise instant that Max opened the door to the stairway landing.

• • •

Back in the Cooler at the Shore kitchen, Josie—furious and suddenly ravenous—slammed a cast iron skillet onto a stove burner. She expertly cracked three eggs and whisked them, as Sal used to describe her cathartic cooking technique, "within an inch of their lives." Faithful Newton, attentive to his mistress's mood yet ever hopeful for scraps, eyed her from a wary distance, emitting a gentle "*bwoof*" as she shaved cheddar curls from an oversized block of cheese.

"You're the best guy I know," she told the dog, offering him a generous helping.

She'd delayed her exit from the party only long enough to ask the Battins to drop Torre off at home later on and then driven home on autopilot, in a fury. Max had been completely unreasonable. He'd jumped to a ridiculous conclusion, then been impossible to placate—as if he'd had any right. But Max was only one of numerous offenders on her "jackass" list at the moment. Other top spots had been allocated to the insufferable Hal Thorn, for rejecting the "paltry" sum she had scraped to save for her son's education; to the holier-than-thou Moses Jones, for assuming the worst about her friendship with Billy; and to the thickheaded Billy himself, for having been so oblivious to his poor wife's plight.

"Men!" she seethed as she flipped her perfect omelet onto a plate. She had had it with each and every one of these clowns.

Eating her eggs with gusto, she was unaware that yet another member of the offending gender was parked across the street from her establishment, watching her through the storefront window.

• • •

Language Arts Journal, February 16 Torre Messina

<u>I feel really glad</u> that mom won that trip to Hawaii the other night. She was sound asleep by the time I got home, right in front of the TV in all her dressy clothes, and I didn't want to wake her up so I didn't even get to tell her until morning. She actually didn't seem as happy as I thought she would be, but she said that was just because she couldn't think of a good time to be away from the deli. I hope she can figure something out because <u>I feel like she could use a vacation.</u>

School has been kind of boring. I like to work ahead sometimes, especially in math, but then I have to wait for everyone to catch up. The only fun part lately is working with Mr. Jakes on his security project for the Department of Education. It's easier than I thought it would be. For people smart enough to make all those tests they sure don't know much about building a computer network that a kid like me can't crack. <u>I feel that's kind of funny.</u>

CHAPTER 11:

The New Jersey ASS

Max sighed and rolled his eyes. He probably should have known better than to ask his Advanced Pre-Calc class why Pi was an irrational number.

"You just can't reason with Pi. It never listens."

"Maybe it's bipolar."

"Maybe it's senile."

"Maybe it has PMS."

"Maybe it's perfectly rational and we're just in denial."

"Yeah, there's two sides to every story."

"Wise guys. You're hilarious." Max only half managed to suppress a smile. He had to admit these kids were pretty funny; it must have come from watching all that TV when they should have been studying. Oh well, Pi Day, March 14, offered a nice diversion from the grinding NJ ASS test prep.

Max drew π on the whiteboard at the front of the classroom, pausing for a moment to marvel at the simultaneous simplicity and complexity of this miraculous mathematical constant, key to so many critical scientific formulae.

"Torre," he called out, defaulting to the one student he knew would give him a sarcasm-free response, "why is Pi an irrational number?"

"Its value can't be expressed as a fraction, and its decimal representation never ends or repeats."

"Precisely." The teacher nodded. "Which implies, among other things, that no finite sequence of algebraic equations—no powers, no roots, no sums—can equal its value. It's a fascinating construct, don't you think?"

Max looked into a sea of blank faces. "Some mathematicians spend their lives trying to understand more about the nature of Pi. Archimedes. Ptolemy. Liu Hui."

"Louis Who-ee?" said a student.

"Liu Hui, third century Wei Kingdom mathematical genius," Max explained. "He—oh for goodness' sake, don't any of you have any curiosity about this?"

"Mr. Moskin?"

"Yes, Persey?"

"What's your favorite kind of pie?"

Persephone wasn't trying to be impudent. Like many students at Country Day, she was focused on the bake sale that Dr. Nobler and Mrs. Luffhauser had organized for later that afternoon. Unlike her peers, Persey wasn't planning to eat anything, but she found that lately she got a vicarious thrill out of imagining the sumptuous goodies others would consume. The Pi Day bake sale would be a spectacular venue for indulging in food voyeurism.

Max threw his hands up in the air. "Okay guys, okay. I get it. Three-point-one-four is a bore, but I spent half of last night compiling a list of riveting facts and theories about Pi. We can either have a discussion about said facts and theories, or we can go back to our Annual Scholastic Survey prep. The test is the day after tomorrow."

The students groaned in unison, and then spontaneously sent up a pleading chant: "Pi, Pi, Pi, Pi, Pi!"

Max grinned. They were evidently sick to death of standardized test prep, too. He was thrilled to have finally persuaded the class to see things his way.

The entire business of statewide testing seemed pointless to Max. He personally knew dozens of kids who would ace the mathematics portion of this test and yet had no idea whatsoever how to actually think about numbers. Take away the calculators students were allowed—in fact, *required*—to bring with them and most would be helpless as babes. In his estimation, math education had gone to hell in a handbasket once some lamebrains with degrees in education had decided to introduce kids to calculators before they could add two plus two in their heads. The kids had become so dependent on the gadgets they couldn't reason their way out of a paper bag.

• • •

Down the hall, Francine Tripper, who rarely agreed with Max about matters of pedagogy, was also nursing a grudge about the time required to prep for the Annual Scholastic Survey—albeit for different reasons. In the English teacher's opinion, the test missed the mark by focusing to such a large degree on rote, uncreative matters such as grammar, syntax, and punctuation. Gritting her teeth, she scribbled two sentences on her own whiteboard:

John threw the ball.

The ball was thrown by John.

"Why is the second sentence passive?" she asked her charges.

"Because John is passive aggressive?" guessed one.

"Because John can't throw for sh—er, for beans?" offered another.

Mrs. Tripper glanced at the wall clock for the thirteenth time in as many minutes. Her day crept when she had to waste valuable time explaining irrelevant, antiquated subjects such as active voice, misplaced modifiers, and sentence fragments. It was time the students could have spent writing in their Organic Language Arts journals while she shopped online at Crate and Barrel. Curse that state exam, she thought, sneaking a peek at her crib sheet on "Commas versus Semicolons." It was all so, so...inorganic.

• • •

As the afternoon wore on, and as the administration of the three-day ordeal that comprised the NJ ASS grew closer by the hour, one would have to look hard to find a single soul at LFCD in a satisfied frame of mind—until, that is, one found the intrepid headmaster.

To say Pi Day was a perennial favorite of Preston Nobler's was as obvious as stating that brides enjoyed wedding days. The head-master was already licking his lips as he swiveled in his desk chair contemplating the order in which he would line up slices of his favorite indulgences: cherry, blueberry, a wedge of lemon pie to cleanse the palate followed by some piquant strawberry-rhubarb, then finally the *pièce de résistance*, chocolate cream. Scratching his chin, he wondered where he would fit in the apple tart. He sup-posed he could begin with it, as—what did Madame Millefleur call it?—an *amuse-bouche*.

He hoped Emily's supply of pies would last long enough to ful-fill his ambitious gastronomic agenda. Then he reassured himself that there would be an ample supply for him, what with all the mothers and students at LFCD that periodically succumbed to odd food-related regimes. This afternoon, for example, he could predict with certainty that Celeste would content herself with pocketing loose crumbs when she thought no one was watching. And Persephone Thorn—well, the way she was going, she would be lucky not to keel over from starvation before the day was out.

Nobler could not for the life of him understand the eating issues that actually compelled people to *stay away* from food. If you were going to have an issue with food, why not have the kind of issue that gave you pleasure—no matter how many times your mother had to let out your pants? Of the Seven Deadly Sins, glut-tony was surely his favorite. However, he had to admit he did succumb on occasion to pride, and even to a *soupçon* of anger when, say, he thought of that insipid Mother Bernadette. But hey, no one could accuse him of sloth, he reasoned. Oh, no. He was the most ambitious and industrious of men. Consider, for exam-ple, all he was doing to ensure that the upcoming NJ ASS results would benefit Country Day in so many ways.

He planned to use the genuine test scores to target the most attractive candidates from among the students who'd attended Diversity Day. These students would be offered scholarships that he was certain they and their families would be unable to resist. Their enrollment, not to mention the substantial good press he was sure would ensue, would significantly up the school's cachet. He would play the race card and win the jackpot.

As for the scores that would be posted for his current students, these would indeed be stellar. Jakes and his young apprentice had recently located the cyberspace pathway that led directly to the Scantron answer sheets, and all of that code was stored on Jakes's computer. It was only a question of intervening at just the right moment: after the original tests had been scored, but before the results were posted. Timing would be everything, but Jakes said he needed only to keep a weather eye on the system to make his move and avoid detection. His confidence level was high.

Nobler was feeling so good he was thinking of placing a call to Mother Bernadette at OLPS. *In fact, why the hell not?* He buzzed Mrs. Chapel.

"Would you please get The Penguin on the line?" he asked.

Mrs. Chapel knew whom he meant. The headmaster, in his friskier moods, sometimes referred to his archrival as if she were a Batman nemesis. He thought the moniker hilarious, even though the updated habit worn by the sisters at OLPS bore little resemblance to the full-length black and white robes sported by nuns of yesteryear.

"Er, are you certain?" she asked. "I mean, well, you know, talking to her sometimes, er, spoils your mood."

"Not today!" he insisted.

Indeed, he engaged Mother Bernadette in a commiserative conversation about the obscene cost of textbooks before circling around to his actual agenda.

"Say, it just occurred to me," he said with studied casualness, "that the Annual Scholastic Survey is just a few days away. I guess you guys have been busy preparing."

"Oh, not so much," Mother Bernadette said. "We feel our students are thoroughly prepared in the course of their usual studies. Our curriculum is strongly rooted in the basics, you know."

Nobler flinched. He didn't believe the old bird for a second. He envisioned that even now the good Sisters of Perpetual Sorrows were rapping sharp-edged rulers across the knuckles of their quaking charges as they drilled vocabulary flash cards.

"Oh, yes, yes, the basics," he mused. "Well, here we take a somewhat more contemporary tack. I think our lifelong learners will have quite an easy time of it. Say, I have an idea," he added. "What say we make a little friendly wager? Let's see whose kids come out ahead."

"A wager? Well, Dr. Nobler, I'm afraid I'm not a betting woman."

Nobler suppressed a snort. Why, if he had a dollar for every Bingo card The Penguin had ever played…

"Oh come on, let's, you know, do it for charity. Something small. Say, five hundred dollars?"

To his delight, Mother Bernadette took the bait. "Oh, well, for charity? All right then. When—that is, *if* our kids score higher, I'll ask you to donate the proceeds to the Monmouth County Board of Catholic Charities. And what would your charity be?"

He was momentarily stumped. It would probably be inappropriate to ask the head of OLPS to write a check to the Country Day Capital Campaign. He searched his soul, such as it was, for a cause other than his own in which he believed. Suddenly he had a divine inspiration.

"The Wild Bay Food Bank," he said. Making a donation to the doyenne of Country Day's pet project would doubtless benefit his own coffers in the long run. The better Emily's mood, the more open the Luffhausers' checkbook was likely to be.

"It's a deal," said Mother Bernadette, "and may God bless you."

Nobler wished Mother Bernadette the same, confident that heavenly blessings were the last thing he would require to win this wager.

• • •

NJ ASS testing day dawned as a perfect "ten." To the east of the peninsula, a warm sun, determined to dissolve the last stubborn snow heaps of winter, poked its head above a placid, sparkling sea. Amidst the shyly budding dogwoods, backyard birds twittered from the highest branches. But in his lofted twin bed, Torre pulled the covers over his head at the sound of his alarm.

The boy hadn't slept well, which he chalked up to a case of nerves. An ace standardized test taker, he told himself he had no reason to be anxious. He'd always scored in the top percentiles of any standardized test he'd taken before, and he ought to be able to repeat his performance. It was just that Dr. Nobler seemed to be putting so much weight on his personal outcome. Just yesterday, the headmaster had clapped him on the back in that slightly creepy way of his.

"There's a lot riding on you, little fella," he'd said, "but I know you'll do us all proud."

It was kind of confusing to Torre. He knew his test-taking achievements were what caught Dr. Nobler's interest in the first place; but realistically, one kid's scores could do only so much to raise a school's average. In any case, he certainly didn't want to let the headmaster down or—heaven forbid—forfeit his scholarship. His mother had been so thrilled to enroll him at Country Day and he'd come to like the place. Most of the kids were pretty cool, if a little stressed out, and he enjoyed being able to take advanced classes that never would have been offered to him at Lower Fawn Middle School.

He really liked some of his teachers, too. Mr. Moskin was a great math instructor, and Mr. Jakes, weird as he was, had given him lots of opportunities to go beyond even what the other computer science students were working on. He'd had a lot of fun advising the teacher on his poker game, not to mention how cool it was to help him find the weak spots in the Department of Education's network. Why, just the other day they'd discovered that a hacker could have potentially altered the NJ ASS answer sheets and fudged the score outcome. Good thing they found the open doors in the system when they did, and that Mr. Jakes was going to alert the DOE.

At his mother's second call, Torre roused himself. He would eat the hearty breakfast he knew she would have prepared for him, and do his very best in the hours of testing to come. With a little luck, he would make everyone proud.

• • •

Josie fed her son three heart-shaped whole wheat waffles with a side of hot Italian turkey sausage, made certain he had two number 2 pencils, and kissed him on the forehead, wondering if perhaps he felt the tiniest bit warm. It would be unfortunate if Torre were coming down with a cold; she wanted him to do his very best on the NJ ASS. But watching him walk toward the awaiting school bus, she brushed her fears aside. Torre was so damned smart she was sure he could do an outstanding job on the exam under any circumstances. When it came to her boy, Dr. Nobler would not be disappointed.

Glancing at her watch, she hurried into her bedroom and scanned her closet for something to wear for the day's mission. For the third time, she was about to meet MaryAnn at the rehab facility and accompany her on an outing.

The first time, a few weeks ago, she and MaryAnn had bundled up and taken a long walk on Sandy Hook. The beachside national park that flanked central New Jersey's eastern shore was beautiful but near desolate in late winter, making it an ideal spot for a recovering recluse to venture back into the wide world. The two women had reminisced about their early years in Wild Bay and discovered that they and their respective boyfriends, Billy and Sal, shared a predilection for romantic interludes under the Wild Bay boardwalk. "It's the one private moment Billy hasn't written a song about," MaryAnn confided. "Must be because I told him if he ever did I would murder him, plain and simple."

The second outing had been to a midday movie playing at a small art house in the trendy town of Red Bank. It starred Paul

Giamatti as a hapless middle-aged ne'er-do-well, and was pretty entertaining. It was sad, too, because it reminded MaryAnn and Josie that they were also growing older. It would take vigilance, they both agreed on the drive back to MaryAnn's facility, to ensure their own lives didn't devolve into existential limbo once their children were gone.

"Makes you want to have a drink, doesn't it?" MaryAnn had said. Then, laughing at the look on Josie's face, she assured her friend that she was only pulling her leg. "Those days are over, Josie," she'd added. "The twins need me, Billy needs me, and most of all, I need me."

Tucking a tailored pale denim shirt into her black jeans, Josie wondered what excursion she ought to suggest for today. Hiding out in solitary parks and darkened movie theatres were good first steps for MaryAnn's gradual reentry to public life, but as her doctors had explained to Josie, soon their patient would have to mingle with others in more routine day-to-day interactions. Josie thought that was just as well; the feeling of hiding in plain sight was spooking her—or *something* was spooking her. In fact, lately she'd been wondering if some of MaryAnn's agoraphobia was rubbing off on her. Now and again she'd had the strange feeling that someone was watching her, even following her. *Crazy me*, she thought, sighing.

Scooping up her handbag and cell phone, she headed out to the Cooler at the Shore van, mentally running through a list of potential destinations to suggest to MaryAnn. *Lunch at that new shopping complex at the pier in Long Branch? Bargain hunting at Marshall's? Yeah, maybe that.* She could use some new bras if nothing else, and she—

"Josie."

She was so engrossed in her thoughts that she didn't hear her name, so the man said it again, louder. "Josie. Jos."

Finally, Josie stopped short. Now that it had registered, she recognized the familiar, deep tone, and the distinct Jersey cadence. She closed her eyes for a moment before allowing them to focus on the man who'd called her name.

"Sal," she said.

CHAPTER 12:

Decisions

April 1

Dear Ms. Thorn:

The Brown Board of Admission has completed its evaluation of close to 20,000 applications for our entering freshman class, a record number. With so many candidates competing for every available spot, our job has been a difficult one. Many of us here at the Admissions Office have not slept well in weeks, perhaps because we had to resort to multiple cups of black coffee, Red Bull chasers, and handfuls of those chocolate-covered espresso beans just to slog through the mountains and mountains of files that, quite honestly, all began to blur together after a while.

Where were we? Oh, yes.

It is with sincere regret that we must inform you that your application is not included among our acceptances. To deny admission, especially to a legacy applicant, is a difficult matter, both for those who will not be joining us next fall and—lest you forget—for us as well. After all, the salary of an admissions officer is hardly Wall Street level, and some of us could have gone to work at Goldman Sachs or JP Morgan, but oh no, we chose another path and now we're both exhausted and unpopular. But I digress.

We understand you may well be disappointed by our decision—crushed, perhaps. We want to acknowledge your many achievements and we hope you understand that, in the end, it is not where you study but what you do with your education that matters. We're sure you'll think of something.

April 1

Dear Mr. Luffhauser:

On behalf of the Harvard Committee for Admission, I am delighted to offer you a place in our incoming freshman class. This year we received more applications than ever before (more than Yale, but who's counting?). With so many exceptional candidates to choose from, we accepted students who not only excelled in academics but also evidenced sterling character and extraordinary accomplishments. How can we determine from a mere sheaf of paper who is truly worthy to attend our illustrious institution? Simple: we're Harvard; we're smart.

We hope you will accept our offer of admission. We will need your decision no later than May 1. But who are we kidding? We all know you're coming. Don't forget your toothbrush.

Should you have any questions for the Admissions Office in the next few weeks, we suggest you consider whether these questions are really worth asking. We are, quite frankly, over it. And we are already busy beating the bushes for next year's record crop of applicants, most of whom we will, of course, deny.

Again, congratulations. May we suggest you buy a lottery ticket? This is your lucky day.

CHAPTER 13:

Fashion Show

Hey Good Lookin'
Please join us on April 10 for a hot, hot, hot
"School's Out For Summer" Preview Fashion Show

at The Bare Bottom Yacht Club

In a few short months, our favorite season will be here.
Come see the newest clothing lines from local vendors
modeled by Little Fawn Country Day moms, daughters,
and faculty

Tickets: $350
(includes a gift bag filled with money-saving coupons!)

All proceeds to benefit the GOK Capital Campaign

Dress: Fabulous

"Persey," Chip said for the hundredth time, "I really mean it. I don't have to go to Harvard. It's just not that big a deal. We can both go to Rutgers. It'll be fun!"

"*Mmmpppfff. Yrrrr prents'll killoo,*" Persephone replied, popping yet another crabmeat canapé past her lips.

"No, no, my parents won't kill me."

In the past ten days, since college decision letters had arrived, Persey had ended her fast with a vengeance. Chip had become expert at deciphering the words that the love of his young life managed to speak between mouthfuls of munchies. They'd had this very conversation several times before, but he couldn't seem to convince Persey that his plan was viable.

They both knew that his parents would not literally kill him if he declined his spot at Harvard, although there was a pretty good chance they might stage a dual suicide to rival *Romeo and Juliet* for sheer drama. At the very least, they would likely disown him and take a pair of scissors to the family photo albums, leaving ragged holes where their erstwhile adored offspring had proudly stood.

"*Dunnwoorra abuffme,*" Persey went on.

"But I *am* worried about you."

Persey had become way too thin during what she'd considered her Gandhi-like quest to bend the powerful forces of the cosmos through hunger striking. At first it had been a relief to see her reverse her stance on food so dramatically, but honestly, Chip thought, he'd never seen anyone eat like this in his entire life. It couldn't be healthy for a person, could it?

"*Passa dewooldeggs?*"

He dutifully passed a platter of deviled eggs, though he did so against his better judgment. At this rate, the hors d'oeuvres that his mother and Josie had laid out backstage at the Country Day fashion show would not last long. It was also highly likely that Persey would no longer fit into the Gottex tankini she'd agreed to model weeks earlier.

"Do you think you should?" he asked as Persey dunked an egg into a bowl of onion dip.

"*S'okay. Zootcums widdacaffen.*"

Even Chip couldn't figure this one out, which forced Persey to take a breath and clarify. "This swimsuit comes with a caftan." She nodded toward a billowy length of fabric hanging behind her. She planned to drape it over herself as she walked down the Bare Bottom Yacht Club dock that would serve as the fashion models' runway.

Chip nodded. He admired his girlfriend's adaptability, if not so much her appetite. If only Persey's mother had taken things as well. Not as resilient as her daughter, Lydia had taken to her bed once the dreaded Brown rejection letter arrived in the mail. So far nothing—not even the delights of a "hot, hot, hot" fashion extravaganza—had been able to rouse her.

Back at the Thorn household, Hal had tried in vain to lure his wife from her state of recline. He had coaxed her with offers of dinners at *La Petite Biche* and even a shopping excursion to the Lilly Pulitzer flagship store on Madison Avenue. He had repeatedly brought in the family pups, Charles and Camilla, to plead with their sad spaniel eyes for "walkies." Still, Lydia languished.

Hal began to feel so bad about this entire damned college business and its impact on his wife and daughter that he almost— although not quite—considered renouncing his plan to collect his Ergo-Geri cash cache in the Cayman Islands and rendezvous with the lovely Carmen in Mexico. Nevertheless, vague feelings of unease (which those slightly more self-aware than Hal might have identified as guilt) provoked in him the need to do something for his soon-to-be abandoned family. He transferred the bulk of the legitimately earned funds in his bank and brokerage accounts into Lydia's and Persephone's names and, for good measure, took out a substantial life insurance policy on himself. *One never knows, does one?*

• • •

Josie watched with an undeniable sense of satisfaction as MaryAnn pulled up to Cooler at the Shore in her new dark gray Volvo station wagon, a gift from her husband in honor of her recent homecoming. Respecting MaryAnn's wishes to blend in, Billy had resisted the temptation to buy his wife something flashier. Since nearly every family on the peninsula had at least one Volvo wagon in their driveway, the vehicle was unlikely to draw any special notice.

MaryAnn looked fresh and pretty in a cream-colored camisole, pale blue Juicy jumpsuit, and espadrilles. Her hair was drawn back in a long ponytail, and her makeup-free visage was adorned only with a pair of medium-sized silver hoop earrings. It was clear to Josie that her friend had worked very hard to blend into the background, but the point was that she was *out*, making her first public appearance among the Country Day crowd since her unceremonious disappearance from the social scene several months back.

Josie had prepared her obligatory food contribution to the fashion show the day before and had Jorge deliver it in the Cooler van so she could ride over with MaryAnn. She'd wanted emotional support this afternoon, and because of recent events, Josie wanted some support herself. She was pleased to have a little time alone with MaryAnn on the drive over to the Bare Bottom Yacht Club, since MaryAnn was the only one she had so far confided in about her ex-husband's return. So far, she hadn't even told Torre that his father was back in town.

MaryAnn and Josie greeted each other with a hug, and it wasn't long before MaryAnn asked what her latest conversation with Sal had yielded. Josie sensed that she was not only genuinely interested in her situation, but was also relieved to take the attention off herself. For her part, Josie was glad to have a confidante. Sal's showing up had thrown her for a loop. Their divorce, filed on grounds of abandonment, had been finalized years ago, and she had never known anything of his whereabouts. At first she had tried to deflect Sal's efforts to talk with her, literally turning on her heel and running from him the first time he approached her, and later refusing to take his many calls. But in the end, she had heard him out. He was Torre's dad, after all. She at least owed it to her son to find out what had brought him back.

"What did he tell you?" MaryAnn asked. "Did he, you know, ask for money like you thought he would?"

She shook her head. "MaryAnn, you won't believe it—it was exactly the opposite. He told me he's flush and that he wanted to *give* us money to pay me back for what he took, and more."

"You believe him?"

"I didn't at first, but I guess he figured I wouldn't. He pulled out an iPad, logged onto Smith Barney, and showed me a portfolio he'd set up in trust for Torre. It was—well, my God, it was this huge amount. It would pay for Torre's college, and grad school too. I still didn't think he was legit, but he gave me his user name and password and I checked it out later on. The money is really there." She had stared at the six-figure sum for a long while, then pressed "Print" and held a hard copy of the portfolio in her hand. She couldn't have been more stunned if Sal had told her he had brought her a unicorn and with the wave of a wand manifested the magical beast in her living room.

"Where did he get it?" MaryAnn asked.

"That's the other unbelievable part," Josie said. As the two women made their way along the winding buttonwood-lined roads that led to the yacht club, she recounted Sal's story.

After cleaning out their joint accounts all those years ago, Sal had wound up in Las Vegas. It hadn't taken him long to lose nearly all the money he'd taken. Down to his last few thousand dollars, he'd finally discovered what kind of gambling he was actually good at: poker.

"All the rest of it is a bunch of sucker's games," Sal contended. "Roulette, craps, baccarat—it's all chance, so you play long enough and the house always wins. But poker is a game of skill. It's not about the cards you get; not really. It's about reading your opponents, about getting the other guys to fold, about bluffing."

Josie had scowled and crossed her arms across her chest, certain he was bluffing at that very moment, but he'd been prepared for skepticism and pressed on.

"Most poker hands never go to a showdown; it's a fact. And even when they do, the guy with the best hand has usually given up already. Look it up. I swear, there are actually academic studies on this stuff."

Josie had shaken her head. "Okay, but what makes you such an expert?"

He had grinned. "I'm better than an expert. It turns out I'm a natural. I won back the money I'd lost, almost to the penny, and that's when it hit me."

"What hit you?"

"I was so good at this. I was *smart*—smart enough to stop playing, to stop gambling. I could make a fortune—in the end I *did* make a fortune—by teaching other people what I knew."

The world of poker had been exploding, Sal went on to explain, thanks to all the new gaming websites. He'd started a school for poker players that soon gained a reputation for turning out champions, and the profits had rolled in.

"That's what you've been doing all this time?" Josie had asked, incredulous. "You've been in Las Vegas *not gambling*?"

"Well, that's what I did until lately. Recently, I decided to do something else. I found out that, well, things in the online poker world are about to change. It's not going to be quite as... lucrative."

"And you know this how?"

"Well, let's just say I have friends."

Josie had raised an eyebrow. She could only imagine what kind of "friends" a man made in Vegas gambling circles. She'd caught a whole season of *The Sopranos* before her cable company had realized they were giving her free HBO by mistake.

"Anyway," he had persisted, "I'm into something else now. The thing is, I missed cooking almost as much as I missed you guys. I opened a new restaurant on the strip, and Josie, it's doing really well. It's a vegetarian restaurant called Las Vegan."

Of everything Sal had told her, this had left her the most agog. Sal, a vegetarian? The Sal she'd known would have been happy to subsist on an all-sausage-and-capocollo diet. Still, she had to admit in spite of herself that her ex-husband appeared extremely fit. He'd dropped a good twenty-five pounds, she'd bet, and he looked as if he'd been working out. In fact, goddamn it, Sal looked better than ever. He hadn't lost a hair on his head, and the gray that sprinkled his unruly locks rendered him sort of Richard Gere-like. In fact—

Nah. She'd shaken her head. *Don't go there, Josie.*

"Las Vegan?" was all she'd said.

"Yeah, it turns out lots of people want to eat healthy these days, but at my place they don't have to eat stuff that tastes like cardboard to do it. Josie, I tell you, we never have an empty table."

Having now surprised his former wife on almost every front, Sal revealed his final card. He wanted to make things up to Josie and Torre, no strings attached. But if Josie could *ever* find it in her heart to forgive him, he wondered if she could possibly give him a second chance. "I miss my family, Jos," he'd implored her. "I know I don't deserve it, but God, I'd give anything to be a part of your lives again."

As Josie and MaryAnn approached the yacht club, MaryAnn pressed her friend for her reaction. "Wow, what did you say to that?"

"I couldn't say a word," said Josie. "It was like when you're having a dream and you want to yell out, but your voice is paralyzed. I mean, here's this guy that just up and left us years ago. Part of me wanted to strangle him, but part of me…"

"Part of you, what?" MaryAnn prompted, pulling her car into the valet parking line. She knew all too well how complicated relationships were, especially when the man in your life had long ago staked out the real estate in your heart forever reserved for your first love.

Josie shut her eyes and rubbed her temples. For the millionth time in the past few weeks, she tried to suppress the sensation that her head was about to explode. "God help me," she said. "Part of me wishes that somehow this might all work out."

MaryAnn nodded and patted her friend on the shoulder. "It's okay," she said. "I get it."

Just then, as she turned her car keys over to the valet, MaryAnn noticed the simultaneous arrival of someone she'd been wanting to have a word with. "Honey," she said to Josie, "can you save me a seat? I'll come inside in a minute."

"Er, sure, okay," said Josie. She watched as MaryAnn hesitated for a moment, then seemed to resolve herself and threaded her way through the crowd. She wondered if her friend had a certain kindergarten teacher in her sights. Instead, she was a little surprised to see MaryAnn flag down young Mindy and her mom.

• • •

Backstage at the fashion show, Marisa slipped into a spaghetti-strapped leopard print Joie sundress, which she was modeling for the high-end local boutique, Haute Stuff. Peering out into the Bare Bottom's bar area, where the guests were enjoying some pre-show liquid refreshments, she experienced a brief shudder of trepidation. She wondered if MaryAnn Stand might not want to have a word with her today. Likewise, Celeste Battin, and perhaps a few other suspicious types as well. Maybe it had been a poor decision to take center stage at an event where only the mothers of Country Day, and none of the fathers, would attend.

Marisa sighed. Things at LFCD had grown dull as of late. Billy Stand offered her no more than curt nods when he dropped Lucy and Harry off at kindergarten. That sweet Hal Thorn had seemed awfully preoccupied on the few occasions on which she'd seen him since their *tête-à-tête* at the Valentine's dance, and Andy Battin had stopped texting her from his far-off ports of call. Now she had to face a crowd she suspected might be less than fully appreciative of just how adorable she looked in her perky little outfit.

Maybe, she thought, it was time to move on. Just the other day she had taken a call from the principal of Our Lady of Perpetual Sorrows. It turned out that one of the OLPS kindergarten teachers would be leaving at the end of the school year and they would need a replacement. At first Marisa had been quite taken aback. "I'm, er, I'm a Presbyterian," she'd stammered, but Mother Bernadette had chortled benevolently.

"Many of our teachers are secular these days, my dear. I'm afraid there aren't a lot of young ladies right now who are willing to take marriage vows to the Church."

Now Marisa was mulling over her job offer, which came, she had been pleased to learn, with a heavenly pay raise. Maybe it was a divine portent.

• • •

The headmaster's attention wandered as a parade of LFCD mothers and teachers strutted down the dock-cum-catwalk to piped-in strands of Right Said Fred's "I'm Too Sexy." *Note to self*, he thought. *Include some male models next year.* Maybe he could lose a few pounds and take a turn.

The LFCD fashion show was an event about which he had mixed feelings for other reasons as well. Its timing was, arguably, less than ideal. Coming as it did ten days after college admissions decisions, the event placed him square in the sights of any mother who was less than pleased with her child's outcome. This year's results had been a mixed bag.

Acceptances from Penn, Colgate, Swarthmore, Duke, and Harvard (thank God for Chip Luffhauser) were feathers in his cap, to be sure. But rejections for students who had their hearts set on other prizes—MIT, Stanford, Yale, and that cursed Brown, for example—stuck in his craw. Yes, Lydia was absent today (thank God for small favors), but he correctly sensed that other disgruntled parents were waiting for the festivities to conclude. Then they could assail him with not so veiled implications that *he* was to blame for their offspring's relegation to schools of lesser standing. He mentally reviewed his stock responses—*abundance of qualified applicants, mustn't take it personally, it's the school's loss in the end*—knowing all the while that nothing he could say would placate them.

Well, what the hell, he thought. When their kids graduated in June, many of these malcontents would be gone. Those with children in lower grades would, in a triumph of hope over experience, shift their attention to the college quests of their younger sons and daughters. Besides, he had several aces up his sleeve as far as Country Day's reputation was concerned. In another month or so, LFCD would be able to boast remarkable NJ ASS scores; and down the road, the school's influx of Rainbow Recruits would surely raise its college admissions success quotient by taking full advantage of Affirmative Action initiatives. Best of all, by next fall, the construction of his new facilities would be well underway, and thanks to his shrewd investment in Hal's IPO, those additions would be even grander than he had first conceived.

He forced his attention back to the fashion show, noting with interest that Miss Markle, although looking splendid, drew an audience reaction about as warm as the Puritans would have showered on Hester Prynne. Then a tap on the shoulder from Mrs. Chapel interrupted him.

"There's a call for you on the club phone," she said. "It's Madame Millefleur, back at school. She says it's urgent."

As Nobler scurried to the Bare Bottom office he wondered what could possibly be so important that the French teacher would call him. Madame Millefleur, who had declined to attend the show on the grounds that only the French knew anything about fashion, was a bit high-strung, to be sure (he recalled how overwrought she'd been during that silly frog escape incident), so he hoped it was nothing.

But it was something.

"*Mon Dieu,* Dr. Nobler! *Les gendarmes sont ici!*" she all but shrieked into his ear. "Zer are men here from zee—zee—Eff-Bee-Aye!"

The what? The who?

"Zee Eff-Bee-Aye—zee federal poleez. Zey have zee search warrant. Zey have taken zee computer of Monsieur Jakes. Zey say eet ees sum-sing about...about...zee online pok-air!"

• • •

Language Arts Journal, May 1 Mindy Battin

My Dad is back. <u>I feel happy!</u>

It all started when MaryAnn Stand saw me at the fashion show and asked me what the h--- I was doing in her house that night she fell down. She said she never ever left the garage doors open and she wouldn't believe me when I said I just happened to be walking by. My mom was looking at me all funny and I kind of lost it. <u>I felt like I might as well tell the truth</u> because so far nothing I was doing had worked anyway.

So I told MaryAnn that I saw on Halloween that my mom's garage door opened her garage door too. And that night when my mom was out at the Christmas party I figured MaryAnn and Billy were out too. And I just kind of <u>felt like snooping around</u>. I really didn't know why.

I guess I started crying then, and my mom apologized to MaryAnn and then she took me home. <u>I felt so embarrassed</u>. We had a long talk and Mom told me I didn't need to worry about getting Billy Stand's attention - that I was such a great singer I could make it without his help. And then I told her that I hadn't been trying to get Billy's attention at all. I just wanted to do anything - like even get caught breaking into someone's house - that might get my dad to come home.

And then there were a lot of phone calls. And now he's here. <u>Me and Lars are really, really glad</u>. I hope he stays.

Language Arts Journal, May 1 Torre Messina

My dad is back. <u>I feel...I feel. I don't know what to feel.</u>

I can't believe it. I really can't. My mom had him come over the other day. It is so weird. I look so much like him.

And as soon as our dog Newton saw him he ran right up to him and gave him one of his big wet kisses, which <u>makes me kind of feel my Dad is okay.</u>

To be continued, I guess. Dr. Nobler wants to see me in his office.

May 3
FROM: Dr. Preston Nobler
TO: All Faculty and Administrative Staff
RE: Recent Events

As you are by now aware, the Federal Bureau of Investigation recently paid a visit to our school and removed a computer assigned to faculty member Benjamin Jakes. I have personally been assured by the FBI that the computer was taken merely as ancillary evidence in a case having to do with possible illegal offshore banking activity by the purveyors of certain online gambling websites. According to federal investigators, Mr. Jakes's school computer was occasionally logged onto these sites (in error, I am quite certain).

Additionally, I have been assured that the investigation does not directly involve anything having to do with Little Fawn Country Day or its academic activities. There is no truth to any rumor to the contrary. There is no reason to be concerned. Indeed it is true I have been visibly perspiring and also shaking a great deal as of late, which I know has fed the fires of speculation. However, I want to assure you all that this is merely a side effect of some allergy medication. It's pollen season here on the peninsula, as you know!

Finally, until we locate Benjamin Jakes, whose temporary disappearance is most likely due to a similar bout of spring allergies, computer science classes are suspended and will be replaced by study periods during which students may independently pursue their lifelong learning objectives.

CHAPTER 14:

Scores

Hal carefully steered his rented Sebring convertible along the winding road that led from Grand Cayman's Owen Roberts International Airport to George Town, trying to concentrate as best he could on keeping to the left. Driving always took added concentration in any of these damned British Crown colonies, and yet the seaside vista was such that he could not keep his attention from wandering a bit. The late afternoon colors were so pure and vivid, they reminded him of shades of Crayolas that his daughter had so loved to draw with when she was little. There was the Lemon Yellow sun, suspended almost cartoonishly above the Turquoise Blue sea. And that sky—what was that color Persey had liked so much? Cerulean. Yes, that was it, cerulean.

A blaring horn tore Hal from his reverie, and a doorless jeep swerved by him in a near miss. *Cheese it with the memories,* he chastised himself. They weren't going to do him any good. Persey would be fine without him, especially now that that nice young Brad was in the picture. Besides, he had important business at hand.

He pulled his car up to the bank where his Ergo-Geri funds were safely stashed and checked his Rolex. He was a few minutes early for his appointment, leaving him just enough time to dash into the men's room and reshape his wind-tousled hair.

Once he re-emerged, satisfied that he looked his usual dapper self, Hal took a seat and accepted a cup of tea from the bank's solicitous greeter, a plump, fusty fellow who reminded Hal a tiny bit of Preston Nobler. Through the glass walls of an office across the room, he eyed the woman with whom he would meet in a few minutes.

Ms. Dominica Pascal was as enticing a banker as one would ever want to meet, and Hal had nursed a crush on her since she helped him open his account two years ago. An angular, almond-colored young lady of indeterminate racial origin, Dominica was every inch the vision of bureaucratic propriety, yet Hal sensed that a smoldering earthiness lurked somewhere just beneath her prim Chanel suit. He had a nose for such things.

Hal let his imagination roam unfettered for a moment as he watched the lovely Ms. Pascal, who was conversing soberly with a thin, bespectacled man sitting across from her. Oddly, he had the feeling he'd seen this man before. *Nah, couldn't be,* he told himself. It was just a coincidence that the guy bore a resemblance to that geeky Country Day computer science teacher.

Whoever this customer was, he certainly didn't look very happy. As Ms. Pascal somberly shook her head, he moved from gesticulating wildly to hanging his own head in his hands. A wave of what looked like sympathy flashed across Ms. Pascal's face, but she swiftly replaced it with a mask of professional composure as she ushered the gentleman from her office. It was then that Hal realized the man was Benjamin Jakes, although Jakes himself was too distraught to notice much of anything as he slumped out the bank's front door.

Encountering someone from Little Fawn Country Day was hardly what Hal had expected in this venue. Was this an inauspicious omen, or merely a coincidence? After all, any number of people might choose to shelter their money in the Grand Caymans for the usual reasons: tax evasion, the locals' indifference as to the source of one's funds, and the bank's general reluctance to divulge information about any "suspicious activities" in which one might have "allegedly" engaged. Still, he couldn't help but feel a tad unnerved—sufficiently so that he almost neglected to flirt with Ms. Pascal as she offered him a seat and tapped away at her computer, processing his request to withdraw the entirety of his Ergo-Geri funds.

Happily, everything appeared to be in order. He began to relax when Ms. Pascal excused herself to have his cashier's check drawn up at the teller window. When she handed him the check, however, all was not well.

"There must be some mistake, Dominica. Take another look, will you, darling?" he asked with what he hoped was a casual, Cary Grant-like insouciance. "This balance is less than half of what's in the account."

Dutifully, the banker accommodated his request. *Tap-tap-tap* went her long, elegant fingers, but *tsk-tsk-tsk* was the sound her tongue made against her pearly white teeth.

"I am so very sorry, Mr. Thorn," she said somberly, "but many of your funds were withdrawn just yesterday."

"What? Who could—how—?" Hal sputtered.

"The funds that were direct deposited from…let me see here…Little Fawn Country Day School. Those were rescinded in full. The transactions were not finalized; they were still callable on demand."

"Jesus, Mary, and Joseph!" spewed Hal, drawing a stern look from Ms. Pascal.

"Mr. Thorn, please, I'll ask you to lower your voice."

"But, but, but—"

Ms. Pascal appraised him frostily. There were apparently no "buts" about it. "If you have a problem with the withdrawals, you will need to take it up with the party in question," she said with a note of finality. "Do you still wish to withdraw the amount that is left?"

He looked at his substantially diminished nest egg; it would simply have to do. He couldn't figure out for the life of him why Nobler had taken his money back—if it was Nobler.

As he exited the bank, his gait far less jaunty than when he entered, Hal went back to wondering if that computer geek had had anything to do with his reversal of fortune. He did not have to wonder for long, because Benjamin Jakes was sitting on a wrought iron bench just in front of the bank, his hands still supporting the weight of his shiny head.

"Excuse me," said Hal. "Don't I know you?"

Jakes raised his watery eyes, which registered vague recognition.

"Hal Thorn," said Hal, thrusting out his hand and smiling by sheer force of habit. "We met at my daughter's school."

"Oh, ah, yes. Of course." Jakes cleared his throat and shook hands. "Uh…may I ask…that is, I mean, what are you doing here?"

"I was just about to ask you the very same," said Hal.

"Well, right now I'm waiting for a damned cab that doesn't appear to be coming. And then…then I'm going to go get drunk."

For a number of reasons, the latter part of Jakes's plan struck Hal as an exceptionally good idea. He could use some alcohol—perhaps a good deal of it—about now. Besides, if he got Jakes loaded, he could find out if he had anything to do with the rescinding of Country Day's funds.

Gesturing to his silver Sebring, which sat glimmering in the sunshine, he offered Jakes a ride to the nearest bar. As the afternoon turned to night, the two, emboldened by alcohol, by fiscal catastrophe, and by the profound joy that came from encountering a kindred spirit who was equally soulless, told one another their respective tales.

Soon Jakes knew about the funds from Hal's bogus IPO, the diminishment of which he had, in fact, nothing to do with. Hal, in turn, learned that Jakes had become so enamored of online poker that he had invested his winnings, along with the rest of his life savings, in an entity that ran several of the lucrative websites. This entity was now under investigation by the FBI for various and sundry racketeering felonies. Unfortunately, all accounts that had received monies from it had been frozen, Jakes's included. The erstwhile teacher was now penniless.

"Woe is us," the two amigos agreed over and over again. (Although they took a somewhat lengthy, gin-inspired verbal detour to debate the possibly more grammatically correct substitution of "Woe is we.")

No one was certain of just how much Tanqueray-and-tonic Hal and Jakes had consumed before they drove off into the darkness—forgetting to turn on the Sebring's headlights, several eyewitnesses later confirmed. But everyone agreed it was a prodigious amount—easily enough to cause Hal, unaccustomed as he was to driving on the left, to steer the convertible off the road and into a jetty at the tip of Rum Point, where it flipped, exploded, and burned, presumably incinerating both its passengers in the wreckage.

•   •   •

Mrs. Chapel nursed a wealth of mixed feelings as she gingerly entered Dr. Nobler's office and shut its heavy mahogany door behind her. As she soberly revealed the unfortunate news of the presumed death of the school's computer science instructor, along with one of its parents, she wondered if her (admittedly brilliant and successful) plan to recover Country Day's Capital Campaign money from Hal's offshore account had resulted in the tragic accident or even perhaps a suicide. *Mea culpa*, she admonished herself. Still, Hal was a thief, a scoundrel, and a real *anguis in herba*—a snake in the grass.

Mrs. Chapel remained ambivalent as she watched Dr. Nobler blanch, reel, and steady himself against his desk. *Don't worry, you jackass, the money is safe*, part of her wanted to tell him, but she decided to let her feckless boss sweat things out for a while.

Nobler was dually devastated by the news about Jakes and Hal. With his old friend Hal dead, his Capital Campaign money must be gone for good. On top of that, with Jakes also gone forever, Nobler's chances of altering the school's NJ ASS scores seemed slim. Just the other day that miserable ingrate Torre had refused to help when he had laid out his plans and explained to the boy that with Jakes missing, Torre himself had to hack into the DOE and do the necessary deed.

The kid kept insisting that as far as he knew, he had only been "doing security work" with Jakes. He said he'd learned his lesson at his former school and would never hack into a system to alter legitimate information again. "Besides, what you want to do would be cheating," the wretched, wide-eyed innocent repeatedly reminded him.

Knowing he had a few aces up his sleeve, Nobler had set up a meeting with Torre's mother, and she was due for it any minute. As distraught as he was by Mrs. Chapel's news, he knew he had to pull himself together.

"Irene," he snapped, "send flowers to the Thorns' house. Something…oh, I don't know, something pastel—wisteria maybe, with a spray of baby's breath. Collect any of Benjamin Jakes's effects immediately, and bring them to me. And Josie Messina is due here any minute. Do not—I repeat, *do not*—speak to her about this before you show her in."

He saw no reason to upset Josie any more than he was planning to upset her already. But when she stormed into his office, with nary a nod to Mrs. Chapel, who could not have had a word with the irate mother if she'd tried, Josie was loaded for bear.

Nobler extended his hand. "Good morning, Mrs. Messi—"

"Don't *good morning* me, you, you—!" Josie froze. Suddenly none of the many epithets she had rehearsed in front of her bathroom mirror seemed even remotely adequate. What words were there to describe a man so vile he would exploit a sweet, brilliant child for such underhanded purposes?

"All right, all right, calm down now. I gather Torre has told you about our little chat." Nobler had kept his master plan a secret from his own mother despite their exceptionally close relationship (Dorothy being such a stickler for "integrity" and other old-fashioned notions), but apparently the distraught Torre had told his mom everything.

"Listen, buster," said Josie, "I always knew you wanted Torre at Country Day for your own selfish reasons, but it's one thing to have a smart kid raise your class average. It's another thing altogether to ask him to commit a felony. You miserable—you—you—you could wreck his entire future!"

"Lower your voice, please," Nobler commanded. He gestured to Mrs. Chapel to leave and shut the office door behind her. "This isn't Wild Bay, after all." He turned to fix Josie with a malevolent stare.

"Don't pretend your little boy is an angel. You were lucky we took him in after that Incident at his last school. We all know he hacked into that computer and changed a bunch of student grades."

"That was a prank to make a point about bullies. Sure, he shouldn't have done it, but this—this is...*criminal*."

"So what?" he parried icily. "Torre has a criminal mind. Remember last fall at the Spaghetti Dinner auction? Don't pretend he didn't steal that bottle of Sauterne."

"He—what? You think he—?"

"And another thing: I have reason to believe he was gambling—yes gambling—via Benjamin Jakes's computer. Yes, yes, I'm quite sure these things can be proven, but there's no need to delve into them, you see. No need at all," he continued in a softer tone. "I just need Torre to help me out with this one little thing. No one will ever be the wiser, and you two can go on about your lives. In fact, I'm sure Torre will ultimately get into a highly selective university, what with his grades and the personal recommendation I'll give him."

This was all too much for Josie. She knew full well who had taken the Sauterne, since MaryAnn had already confessed to her. She also knew about all Torre's "extracurricular activities," and that the sleazy Benjamin Jakes had drawn him into his web. This was a clear case of abuse of power. No one would hold Torre accountable for any misdeed—would they? No. No! She'd make damn certain they wouldn't.

"I don't know what you're trying to pull here, mister, but I'm not going to put up with this...this extortion."

"Now, now, don't make any decisions in the heat of the moment that you might regret. Give that Mediterranean temperament a chance to simmer down," he oozed. "I'd think carefully if I were you."

Josie seethed. "Oh I'll be doing some thinking, all right," she said. As she marched out of the headmaster's office through the maze of corridors that led out of Little Fawn Country Day, she was thinking of just who might be able to help her and her son now. *Let's find out exactly who Sal's friends are,* she thought, *and see what they can do.*

. . .

Nobler was beginning to have an uneasy feeling in the pit of his stomach, and this morning it was more than the aftereffects of his typically generous breakfast. In the ten days that had passed since his meeting with Josie Messina, the woman—to his genuine surprise—had not reneged on her stubborn refusal to let her son become his willing accomplice. In fact, Torre had been absent from school with a "virus" for all this time, although his teachers informed Dr. Nobler that the boy was dutifully keeping up with his assignments, e-mailing them in from home.

Nobler worried that he might be running out of time. He had tried repeatedly to ascertain from the Department of Education exactly when the NJ ASS scores would be released, but to no avail. State employee cutbacks were ubiquitous, and the odds of having a voicemail returned decreased with each new money-saving mandate.

As it turned out, he did not have to wait much longer to find out when the test scores had been posted. As he looked up from his desk, he saw Mrs. Chapel trying in vain to prevent his arch-nemesis, The Penguin, from entering his sanctuary.

Clutching a printout of the standardized test scores in her hand, Mother Bernadette began to wave it triumphantly. "Pay up, pal," she said with what appeared to be a tad less humility than was seemly for a woman of her vocation. "I win."

An event such as this, in and of itself, would have marked a low point in Nobler's day, but for one thing: Mrs. Chapel was equally ineffective in preventing an additional set of visitors from breaching his domain. These gentlemen also brandished papers, albeit of a different sort.

"Excuse us, Sister." One of the blue-suited men nodded reverently to Mother Bernadette. "Forgive this intrusion, but we have some urgent government business to conduct. Sir, are you Preston Nobler?"

"Wha…uh…who wants to…er, that is, yes, yes I am."

The speaker opened a wallet and flashed a badge.

"Federal Bureau of Investigation. Sir, you are under arrest."

CHAPTER 15:

Commencement

June 10
FROM: Mme. Yvette Millefleur, Acting Headmaster
TO: All Faculty and Administrative Staff
RE: Graduation

Despite any rumors to the contrary, Upper School graduation will take place as planned on June 15 on the Little Fawn Country Day athletic field, rain or shine (if rain, bring your *parapluie*).

We ask you to strongly encourage students of all grades, and their parents, to attend, as a show of support for our graduates in this time of—*quel est le mot?*—uncertainty.

Merci beaucoup.

Commencement Day was a scorcher. All along the long rows of folding chairs set up for the occasion, the mothers and fathers of Country Day fanned themselves with their programs. The effect of the undulating motion was so turbulent that Madame Millefleur, Acting Headmaster, had to steady herself against her podium to keep from feeling *un peu* seasick.

"Commence-zement...*ment*...*ment*," she enunciated into the reverberating microphone, "eez a beginning...*ning*...*ning*... *ning*."

Despite the heat, and the palpable frizzing effect it was having on her hair, Lydia could not help but smile broadly as she cast a sidelong glance at her daughter, who was seated among the seventy-five graduating seniors poised to collect their diplomas. Doubtless, those watching Lydia thought she was simply putting on a brave face; after all, it had been only a few weeks since she'd learned Hal's tragic fate. But Lydia had two very good reasons for cheer, though she had to keep them to herself.

The first reason concerned Persey. Although she was not going to Brown, she was bound for the pinnacle of academe: Harvard. She wouldn't have to take any boring old seminars either, for she would be going to Cambridge as the bride of Country Day's valedictorian, Chip Luffhauser. (Lydia knew there would be an awkward moment when the happy couple broke the news of their recent elopement to Chip's family, but in Scarlett O'Hara fashion, she promised herself she would think about that tomorrow.)

Lydia would have to guard her second secret on an indefinite basis. It turned out Hal was alive and well in Mexico after successfully staging his faux car crash with the help of the inventive Benjamin Jakes. In a sincere attempt to alleviate his family's grief—and an equally sincere effort to petition for part of the life insurance money they'd collected—Hal had covertly contacted his wife shortly after his disappearance (and after learning that the lovely Carmen had grown tired of waiting for him in Zihuatanejo and found romance with a well-to-do condominium developer in Ixtapa). Although relieved for Persey's sake that Hal was still on the planet, Lydia had wished him and his new business partner Mr. Jakes well, while opting to keep the insurance payout for herself. After all, she would need to buy adorable outfits for her future grandchildren.

In the row behind Lydia's, Emily rolled her graduation program into a cylinder and swatted a fly. She was feeling sour; Chip had been acting strangely as of late, and she and Brad had barely spent any time with their son as he approached this life milestone. Chip had even declined the elaborate graduation party his parents had begun to plan, asking instead if they could put the funds aside in a "little nest egg." Very odd, indeed.

On top of that, this ugly business with the recently indicted Dr. Nobler was a nightmare. Under no circumstances would Emily continue to send the younger members of the Luffhauser brood to the scandal-tainted Little Fawn Country Day. But in light of a recent development at OLPS—namely, the parochial school hiring the infamous Marisa Markle—she was not so certain that option would prove a wise choice. As Madame Millefleur waxed on, Emily pondered another course of action. Yes, yes, it could work. She would have to speak to Brad, and they would have to move quickly.

After the acting headmaster's speech, all were invited to stand for "The Star-Spangled Banner," as sung by "zee leetle songbird, Mindy Battin." Many in the crowd winced and braced themselves, but Mindy did a credible job, especially in the opinion of her recently returned father Andy, who stood proudly clasping the arms of Celeste and little Lars as Mindy trilled her patriotic opus. Beaming at the darling girl, from whom he now realized he'd stayed away too long, Andy marveled at her talent. He was only sorry he could not fully appreciate it, as his hearing had been permanently damaged when his eardrum burst during a badly pressurized landing in Kuala Lumpur.

Finally—and not a moment too soon for the majority of wilted onlookers—the senior class of Little Fawn Country Day marched up one by one to receive a sheepskin and a handshake from Madame Millefleur. The Country Day community hailed each one with loud and enthusiastic cheers, and only the most careful of observers would have noted the absence of a few voices.

Missing from the festivities was, of course, former headmaster Preston Nobler, who was awaiting trial on embezzlement and tax fraud charges. In the end, the Feds had been unable to pin him for tampering with the NJ ASS results, since the execution of his carefully contrived plan had never come to fruition. Nor were they able to tie him to online gambling racketeering charges, for he had no entanglement with the miscreants they were targeting on those counts. Nevertheless, while certain offshore banking records in Grand Cayman were investigated, law enforcement authorities had noticed a trail of money from Little Fawn Country Day's Capital Campaign account to a fund that had clearly been part of a Securities and Exchange fraud perpetrated by the late Hal Thorn. Moving money raised for a non-profit cause to an offshore account, let alone one associated with an investment scam, was not strictly legal, as it turned out. To be precise, it was a flagrant violation of the tax code, section 501c.

Also absent from the graduation festivities were Torre Messina and his parents. Mother, father, and son were on a United Airlines flight to Hawaii even as the graduates tossed their mortarboards into the air; they would use the trip Josie won at the Valentine's raffle as a chance to get reacquainted as a family. To Torre's delight, Josie had begun to look at Sal in a new light when she'd learned that his "friends" were not shady organized crime figures after all, but rather the very authorities whose legwork had landed Nobler in custody. The reformed Sal was now affiliated with the good guys. What's more, with re-marriage to Josie pending, Sal was determined to heed her warning that she would kick him to the curb if he ever again did her wrong.

Seated three across on that United 727, the Messinas made a handsome tableau. As Torre dozed in the window seat, Sal and Josie held hands, gazing at the tousle-haired boy who so resembled his dad.

"Penny for your thoughts," said Sal to Josie.

"I hope I packed enough sunscreen," she replied. "Plus, I was thinking…where should Torre go to school next year?"

EPILOGUE: BACK
TO SCHOOL AGAIN

Deeply inhaling the invigorating September air, Principal Max Moskin stood proudly at the entrance of the Wild Bay Charter School. It was, for now, a humble edifice, quickly constructed on the lot adjacent to the Wild Bay Food Bank, and so small it had to be supplemented with several double-wide trailers temporarily converted into additional classrooms. But all that would change soon enough. The funds from Brad's many business connections were pouring in; charter schools had become the *cause célèbre* of the hedge fund crowd. The huge donations from Billy and Moses hadn't hurt, either. Along with much-needed cash, the rockers had infused a certain invaluable "coolness" quotient to the fledging project.

The monetary resources of WBCS were hardly the most impressive thing about it. Far more important, Max knew, was the institution's singular mission. In a world where so many schools had been transformed into standard-free feel-gooderies, Wild Bay Charter would bring back the basics, grounding students firmly in reading, writing, and arithmetic so that, in time, innovation could be built on a sturdy foundation.

"Demanding effort and accountability from all, and substituting earned excellence for self-inflating accolades," the prospectus had read, and Max was determined to stay true to those words.

On the first day of school, the newly anointed principal allowed himself the honor of greeting every student personally. There were Mindy and Lars Battin, being dropped off by their dad. Like so many others in their crowd, the Battins had wholeheartedly embraced the Wild Bay Charter School once they heard the Luffhausers, not to mention the Stands, were behind it. There were Troy Jackson and Juanita Sanchez, two of the many

"Rainbow Recruits" who had declined an invitation from Little Fawn Country Day in order to attend WBCS instead.

There were the Stand twins, little Lucy and Harry, each first grader holding one of their mother's hands. MaryAnn wouldn't be far from her children today or any day; re-certified as a guidance counselor, she had agreed to join the charter school's staff. (It would keep her happily occupied, MaryAnn had told her best friend Josie, while Billy and Moses reunited with their old bandmates to cut their much-anticipated reunion album, *Lessons*.)

And there were Torre and his old friend Josh from Lower Fawn, accompanied by Josie. The sweet smile and demure wave Josie gave Max tugged at his heartstrings just a little, but he was genuinely glad to see her family together again, and he was full of hope about his own future. Max had been so busy and excited about his new job over the summer that he had lost twenty pounds, and he'd noticed already how well single moms were responding to his streamlined physique and his restored confidence.

As the last students filed in, Max embarked on his plan to stop in every classroom and greet each faculty member. He prided himself on having assembled the best and the brightest educators in the county, several of whom had counted themselves among the Little Fawn Country Day "Resistance"—the coterie that had failed to see the logic of Dr. Nobler's academic approach.

On his way to his first classroom, Max stopped briefly at the office to check in with the school's chief administrator, Irene Chapel. Once her role in rescuing her former school's Capital Campaign funds had become clear, Mrs. Chapel was hailed as a hero at Little Fawn Country Day. But she had had quite enough of that snooty old place, thank you very much, she told Principal Moskin during her interview, and she would be happy to bring her knowledge and experience to the Wild Bay Charter School if Max would but grant her one favor. He had happily agreed to let her teach an elective Latin class as she'd requested.

"Good morning, Mrs. C," Max boomed. "A glorious day, isn't it? How on earth does the weather know to turn just a shade crisper after Labor Day?"

"It's a mystery," she offered, smiling.

"Well, I see you're hard at work as usual. I'll let you get back to whatever marvel of efficiency you're accomplishing." He gave his chief administrator a thumbs-up and a wink.

Mrs. Chapel had a good deal of paperwork to attend to, and she was eager to get to it shortly, but first she wanted to make a few final entries in the journal she'd kept during her tenure at Little Fawn Country Day. She had no idea what had possessed her to start it, but there it was, a chronicle so intriguing that— who knew?—with a few clever tweaks, it could transform into that screenplay she could work on after her retirement.

Really, she thought, *who could have foreseen the way things worked out?*

In getting to know the good sisters at Our Lady of Perpetual Sorrows, Marisa Markle had experienced a spiritual revelation and taken preliminary vows as a nun.

Preston Nobler was released on bail, pending his confinement to house arrest under the custody of his mother. Somewhat disoriented by what Dorothy insisted was his continuing dependence on allergy medication, he had taken to calling himself Albus Dumbledore. He insisted he had to find Harry Potter and save him from Lord Voldemort before it was too late.

Josie and Sal had been so successful at launching Las Vegan at the Shore that they were opening a third emporium. Las Vegan Cambridge would run in partnership with Persey Luffhauser. The newlywed had discovered, to her and Chip's great delight, that she could eat an awful lot of this vegetable stuff and still keep her figure—at least until the baby started to show.

"Boy oh boy, you couldn't make this stuff up," Mrs. Chapel murmured to no one in particular.

Throughout the corridors, two long start-of-session bells clamored. Wild Bay Charter School's first day was officially underway. Knowing it was time to attend to the many bureaucratic matters at hand, Mrs. Chapel concluded her scribbles with a few final words.

"*Acta est fabula,*" she said aloud. She smiled, toggling her pen shut with a click. "That's all she wrote."

ABOUT THE AUTHOR

Arlene Matthews is the author of numerous non-fiction books, and appeared three times as a guest on Oprah. She runs a college admissions consulting service in New Jersey.